# A Killing in Dogwood

**By Bill Shuey**

*Victoria,*
*Best Wishes*
*Bill Shuey*
*6/20/20*
*Shepperd F7B*

**Other books by Bill Shuey**

*A Search for Israel*

*A Search for Bible Truth*

*Unholy Dilemma – A Search for logic in
the Old Testament*

*Unholy Dilemma 2 – A Search for logic in
the New Testament*

*Unholy Dilemma 3 – A Search for logic in
the Qur'an*

*Have a Good Week – Ten years of
ObverseView Musings*

*East of Edin*

*Retribution*

The opinions expressed in this manuscript are solely the opinions of the author. The author has represented and warranted full ownership and/or legal right to publish all the materials in this book. This is a work of fiction, some names, places, and identifying details have been changed and real individuals used in a fictitious manner.

# A Killing in Dogwood

ISBN 13: 978-1986248044
ISBN 10: 1986248046


Printed in the United States of America

The worst part of being abused is the betrayal. The ones who should have protected you are the ones who harmed you.
Anonymous

The reality is the greatest risk factor in being a victim of child abuse is being a child!
Anonymous

# Dedication

This book is dedicated to all those missing and exploited children, and their parents, siblings, and extended families.

# Acknowledgements

As with my earlier literary efforts, the team is what makes the endeavor come together – not just the author.

My sister-in-law, Bern, proofread the book twice and was instrumental in correcting the prose for grammar and punctuation.

And to April Wade who gets the last word on punctuation and syntax. Thanks for making it a better product, kid.

And last but never least, my wife Gloria who is always supportive of my efforts and this was no exception.

# Chapter 1

It was the summer of 1956 and the St. Louis Hawks had been dispatched from the National Basketball Association playoffs by the Fort Wayne Pistons three games to two. The Hawks had managed to defeat the Minneapolis Lakers two games to one to advance to the second round. The great George Mikan retired after his Lakers were beaten in the initial round of the playoffs. Unfortunately, the exploits of Jack McMahon and Bob Pettit would be derailed until the next season.

Our beloved Saint Louis Cardinals were mired in the doldrums and on their way to a mediocre 76 - 78 record and a fourth-place finish. Stan Musial was having his normal good year. Lindy McDaniel was throwing blazing fastballs. Joe Cunningham was making dazzling plays, and Al Dark was steady and dependable. Gussie Bush owned the Cardinals and Fred Hutchinson was the manager. Ken and I hoped that our Dad would take us into the ·city to watch a ballgame.

We had grown up listening to the Saint Louis Browns on the radio when we lived on the farm and visualizing in our mind's eye the exploits of Clint Courtney,

Vick Wertz, Satchel Page, and Don Larson who would go on to pitch a perfect game in the 1956 world series for the hated New York Yankees against the Brooklyn Dodgers. Unfortunately, the Browns sold the franchise in Saint Louis and moved to Baltimore to become the Orioles in 1954. We felt betrayed but recovered quickly and changed our loyalty to the Cardinals.

My younger brother and I were spending the summer of 1956 fishing in a small creek, shooting off firecrackers, riding our bicycles, shooting crows, and playing Indian ball. We had just moved into the big town of Dogwood, population 1,001, from our farm at Jake's Prairie and were becoming accustomed to indoor plumbing and the wonders of city life. On Christmas of 1955, my Dad had given me a Mossberg semi-automatic .22. I say my Dad because my Mother didn't think I needed the rifle and, even though she didn't use the words, probably thought I didn't have enough sense to use it safely.

Our fishing consisted of catching a few crickets and then fishing in one of two wonderful fishing holes: a pond in a field across the road from our house and a small creek which ran through the same little farm. We caught a few little sunfish from time to time but that was about the extent of our catch. Much of our time was spent walking from our home on Maple Shade Road to the junction of the new I-44 to buy firecrackers at a firework stand which stood at the change-over from Route 66 and I-44. The ladyfinger firecrackers were about twenty-five cents or so for a string of fifty and we would shoot them all off before we got back home.

Our mother had a Mason jar full of silver dollars and we would take a dollar from time to time to purchase .22 shells and firecrackers. This seemingly inexhaustible revenue source worked well until Mr. Wilkerson, who owned the local dry goods store became suspicious and called our mother. The jig was up, and we paid. Or more likely, I paid, because Ken was never faulted for anything by our mother. The exact penalty paid doesn't come to memory right now.

Our crow hunting expeditions consisted of going into the woods of the farm across the road, sitting still, and waiting for an unsuspecting crow to alight on a limb within shooting range. If we were fortunate enough to kill the first crow, we would hang him from a tree branch and shoot his family members as they landed to check on him. This would go on until we ran out of .22 shells. Since we missed more crows than we hit, the adventure rarely lasted more than an hour or two.

Indian ball was a game we played most every day in good weather. We would ride our bikes from the house to the city ballpark, use second and third bases as our foul lines and proceed to play the game. Only four players are required for Indian ball: one pitcher and one hitter on offense and one infielder and one outfielder on defense. The game was simple. If a ground ball was fielded cleanly by the infielder it was an out and if a fly ball was caught by the outfielder, it was an out. Everything else was considered a hit. The summer of 1956 was consumed with Indian ball. We would start playing at mid-morning and play until the late afternoon. Who won and who lost was of little importance. Ken and I were honing our skills in preparation for playing for the Cardinals when we got old enough. Unfortunately, Ken didn't throw hard enough or run fast enough and peaked out after an outstanding college career pitching for the Rolla School of Mines in Rolla, Missouri. And as for me, well, I was probably good enough, but I couldn't control my emotions or handle any amount of failure. I played with a men's semi-pro traveling team at age fourteen and led the team in most every offensive category. But I would go three for four and sling the bat when I made the one out. I also led the team in being a spoiled jerk. Both of Ken's sons played major college baseball and the older son made it to the Major League and stuck around for ten years; no small feat given his chronic hip problems.

When we weren't busy with other activities and when it was miserably hot, Ken and I would ride our bikes out Highway 19 to the Meramec River and spend the afternoon jumping off a riverbank into a swimming hole. Unfortunately, or perhaps fortunately, we could never get the Reeves girls, Eva and Lillian, to accompany us to the river. But since their home was on the way and young boys' hope springs eternal, we would stop and ask during every trip to the river. I digress. This is about the summer of 1956, the long hot summer during which Johnny Blue Lambert disappeared and turned the town of Dogwood on its ear and some of the residents into semi-insane vigilantes.

# Chapter 2

The last time Johnny Blue had been seen was by Mrs. Shuler who owned the Dogwood Hotel. She told the police that she had seen Johnny Blue walking down the sidewalk of Route 66, minding his own business, throwing rocks at birds, and headed towards his home. Johnny Blue was eight years old, probably too young to be allowed to wander around without adult supervision, but this was rural Missouri during the 1950s. What was the worst that could happen? After Johnny Blue had waved at Mrs. Shuler he seemed to have just disappeared into thin air.

Johnny Blue's family wasn't Dogwood's finest, or on the social page, but no one really suspected them of doing anything to harm the child. After all they had three other children, all younger, and they were well cared for and happy.

When Johnny Blue didn't come home before dark, Mrs. Lambert was irritated but her annoyance turned to concern as the evening turned into night. When Johnny Blue still wasn't home at 9 PM she called Doc Jones, the city marshal, at home and frantically told him that her Johnny Blue hadn't come home, and she feared something had happened to him. Doc drove around town for thirty minutes or so and shined his spotlight in likely spots for a kid to be hiding or walking through and saw nothing. He then went to the Lambert home and talked to Jack and Betty Lambert, Johnny Blue's parents. Jack was trying to calm Betty without a great deal of success and the arrival of Doc only made her more frantic and fearful. After talking to the Lamberts, Doc decided to call Johnny Dills, the county sheriff, and let him know what was happening.

Around midnight, search parties were organized using county deputies and a few citizen volunteers. Early the morning after Johnny Blue's disappearance, more volunteers were called in to aid with the search and every vacant house, garage, outhouse, and doghouse was searched without success. Dogwood wasn't a very large town and the initial search took only the better part of one day. The next day, the search was expanded after the Missouri State Highway Patrol Criminal Investigators were notified and showed up to take control of the investigation from Doc Jones and Sheriff Dills. The state investigators set up roadblocks on the two roads that came into Dogwood: Route 66 from the East and West and Highway 19 from the North and South.

Every automobile and truck were searched, and the trunk of every vehicle was opened. The 1950s were a little different than today and if law enforcement asked you to open your vehicle trunk you did so. After a day of fruitless searches of vehicles, the state investigators turned their attention to the homes and vehicles that were parked in driveways. They mounted a house by house interview of every resident in the town and asked each one to open their automobile trunk to make sure that Johnny Blue hadn't crawled in for some unknown reason. All in all, this initiative consumed three more days and turned up absolutely nothing.

Next the state investigators began rounding up the riff raff, town drunks, and a mentally challenged fellow. They were all interrogated for hours and nothing was learned. It was as if aliens had come through Dogwood and snatched Johnny Blue for some type of weird medical experiment or something. There was no demand for ransom: and if there was, the Lamberts barely had enough money to buy groceries every month. The kids were wearing hand-me-downs and glad to have them. Obviously, whatever had happened to Johnny Blue had nothing to do with kidnapping for ransom.

The state investigators were stumped. Doc Jones was stumped from the get-go as his exposure to crime consisted of an Inspector Clouseau investigation to discover which teenage boys were committing vandalism. He never managed to identify them but had an idea who the perpetrators were. Doc Jones had never been through any type of law enforcement or criminal investigation training and was completely out of his depth from day one of the disappearance.

The state investigators packed up and left after a couple weeks of fruitless inquiries and searches. The Federal Bureau of Investigation refused to get involved because there was no evidence that the child had been abducted for ransom or taken across state lines into Illinois, Oklahoma or any other state that bordered Missouri. In fact, there was no evidence of anything. The child had merely vanished without a trace.

\*\*\*\*\*\*\*\*\*\*\*\*\*\*\*\*\*\*\*\*\*\*\*\*\*\*\*\*\*\*\*\*\*\*\*\*\*\*

The days wore on and life began to return to normal. The old men gathered at Quail Kunkel's barbershop and opined endlessly regarding who had taken the child and why. No one had any information, but it seemed everyone had a theory, a reason for the abduction, and why the body had never been found. Jeff Kunkel, no relation to Quail, thought that some satanic cult had come through Dogwood on Route 66, saw the kid walking down the sidewalk, and seeing no other cars or people, stopped and snatched him so that they could put him on a rock slab and cut his heart out. The Reverend Derwood Jones, no relation to Doc, thought that there was so much evil in the world that someone or something had snatched the child and killed him just for fun. John Smittens felt that some Negro who had inadvertently gotten off the new I-44 and onto Route 66 out of habit had come through Dogwood, saw the child walking down the street, and snatched him to sacrifice to some ancient African god or goddess. Donny Sullivan, who was always good for a head shaking chuckle, opined that he had heard on KMOX radio out of Saint Louis that there had been several UFO sightings and just perhaps some alien culture had beamed Johnny Blue up into their spacecraft and whisked him away to do scientific studies to see if our planet was worth the bother. Such were the conversations, some of which were nutty but provided for speculation and endless discussions.

The same conversations with other individuals consumed the discussions at the Midway Restaurant and Dogwood Café when the men of the town met for morning coffee. The morning conversations might have been slightly more refined and intelligible but some opinion concerning the disappearance of Johnny Blue was always on people's minds and never far from their lips.

# Chapter 3

Vic Clary owned the Stag beer distributorship, John Brummett owned the IGA Supermarket, Royal Knight owned a large vineyard just before Maple Shade Road intersected with Route 66 going towards Saint Louis, Doctor Frank Elders was the family doctor for most everyone in Dogwood, Wilber Mortimeyer managed the Meramec Ice and Fuel Company, Eileen Earls owned the Midway Restaurant and Greyhound bus stop. They, and several other civic minded citizens of Dogwood contributed to a fund for information leading to the identification and capture of the individual(s) who had abducted Johnny Blue Lambert. All in all, the reward money totaled more than $5,000.00 and seemed to be growing. In the 1950s $5,000 was a fair piece of change considering that most working people made less than $100.00 a week at that time.

I knew each of the luminaries who headed the fund-raising effort through my father. Royal Knight was some official in the Eastern Star with my mother and she landed me a job at his vineyard pruning grapes. The work wasn't particularly hard but after snipping a few hundred old vines my right hand was covered with blisters. The first day during lunch Mr. Knight noticed the blisters on my hand and offered to show me how to get some relief. He opened each blister with his pocketknife and then had me soak my hand in dill pickle brine for about ten minutes. The stinging of the brine wasn't fun, but I had to admit that it toughened up the skin and allowed me to keep working which was probably his major interest.

John Brummett was my favorite person when I was younger and living on the farm. We would come into town every other Saturday to purchase groceries. Les Collins' store stocked the most basic of necessities and gasoline but everything else had to be purchased in Dogwood at the IGA foodliner. I developed a game plan which worked most of the time. When Mom went into the store aisles to find items on her list, I would get Ken and we would hang around the drink box which was right inside the entrance. Often Mr. Brummett would see us standing there and feel some compassion for two little boys that rarely got a treat and buy us a Nehi soda: cream for me and grape for Ken. If you are going to silently beg, you might as well be choosy.

Doctor Elders was our doctor for most things while we were on the farm and after we moved into town. In fact, he removed my tonsils when I was about nine in a small surgery suite just off his office. It has been sixty-five years since that experience, and I can still remember him telling me to be still and seeing him placing an ether rag over my nose. My last thought was that the ether smelled good. When I woke up, my mother was feeding me ice cream. For less specialized things, like the flu for example, I would be taken to Doctor DeLeo who was an osteopath and believed 100% in the new wonder drug, penicillin. I learned early on to hide a slight sickness because if I complained I would receive a shot in the back of my front by Doctor DeLeo. After a few of those trips I would have kept a bubonic plague infection to myself!

Wilber Mortimeyer was my Dad's boss at Meramec Ice and Fuel when he drove the bottled gas truck and later the beer truck. In fact, Mr. Mortimeyer gave me my first summer job making 500-pound blocks of ice in the ice plant. In addition to making ice, I had to drag them into the freezer after they froze in the containers and cut the blocks into smaller sizes when people came to purchase ice. It was a nice cool summer job.

Eileen Earls was an older woman and I only knew her by sight. But her son Troy Earls owned the Chevrolet dealership in Steeleville, Missouri, and was one of my

Dad's bowling buddies. Dad loved to tell the anecdote concerning him and Troy going out for a few brews after a bowling tournament in Rolla, Missouri.

I guess Troy got a snoot full and was weaving somewhat on Route 66 coming back to Dogwood. And wouldn't you know it; they got pulled over by a Missouri Highway Patrolman just out of Rolla. The patrolman gave Troy a field sobriety test, which he failed and then loaded him in the patrol cruiser. The patrolman told Dad to drive Earls' car and follow him. With that he took Troy to the night magistrate hoping he would lock him up for the night and fine him for drunk driving. Dad was sitting in the gallery and when the judge asked the highway patrolman if he had Mr. Earls' automobile towed in for impoundment, Dad stood up and said "Judge, the patrolman ordered me to drive Troy's car into Rolla and I was much drunker than Troy." The judge looked at the highway patrolman and just shook his head, dismissed the charges, and suggested that Troy and Dad go across the street and have a few cups of coffee before they took off again.

In a small rural community, everyone knew everyone to some extent and the highway patrolman was sure to remember Dad after that night.

\*\*\*\*\*\*\*\*\*\*\*\*\*\*\*\*\*\*\*\*\*\*\*\*\*\*\*\*\*\*\*\*\*\*\*\*\*\*\*

The fundraising committee held a meeting and after some discussion it was decided that part of the reward money, in fact about $2,000.00 would be used to hire a private detective from Saint Louis whose name was Emil Scaffart. Scaffart was reputed to be the best private eye in the city and could find anyone who was lost. Scaffart supposedly had the uncanny ability to solve any mystery.

Scaffart came to Dogwood and took up residence at the Dogwood Hotel and began sniffing around and asking questions. After two weeks of being a general nuisance, he had discovered nothing, and the good citizens of Dogwood got nothing of substance for their donations to the reward fund. Well that's not entirely true. Mrs. Shuler got her donation back plus some extra for the two weeks rent of one of her fine rooms in the Dogwood Hotel. And the Midway Restaurant turned a few bucks off the three-square meals that Mr. Scaffart managed to work into his busy schedule of searching for clues in the disappearance of Johnny Blue. Other than this meager return of investment, plus whatever Scaffart bought from the Dogwood package store to keep him fortified and other incidentals purchased from town businesses, nothing of any real value was gained from his investigation. Certainly, Dogwood was no closer to discovering what had happened to Johnny Blue.

Why anyone would think that a private detective would have more success figuring out what had happened to Johnny Blue than state investigators was anyone's guess. Everyone who donated to the fund was entitled to a voice and vote, so I suppose the majority were just grasping at straws when no solution was at hand. Anyway, Mr. Scaffart went back to Saint Louis the richer. And neither the committee members nor the community in general were any more the wiser regarding what had happened to Johnny Blue.

\*\*\*\*\*\*\*\*\*\*\*\*\*\*\*\*\*\*\*\*\*\*\*\*\*\*\*\*\*\*\*\*\*\*\*\*\*\*

After the failure of Mr. Scaffart to make any discovery regarding the child's disappearance, someone had a bright idea that a noted clairvoyant who practiced in Kansas City, Missouri, under the name of Mother Astoria might be able to help find the child. Over the very vocal objections of Brother Daniel Lee Jamison who tended to the flock at the Holiness Temple in Christ just outside of Dogwood, it was decided to bring

Margaret Temperin a/k/a Mother Astoria to Dogwood in an attempt to provide some closure for the Lambert family and the community at large.

\*\*\*\*\*\*\*\*\*\*\*\*\*\*\*\*\*\*\*\*\*\*\*\*\*\*\*\*\*\*\*\*\*\*\*\*\*\*\*\*\*

A genuine psychic is someone with extra sensory perception (ESP). Those with ESP can 'read' or sense things most of us are unable to detect. Most people who claim to be clairvoyant see the future about as well as Mr. Magoo, but that doesn't deter people from giving them money. Most thinking people attribute little if any value to psychics. In fact, most people just read the Jeane Dixon horoscopes in the newspaper for fun while placing little if any significance to her predictions.

\*\*\*\*\*\*\*\*\*\*\*\*\*\*\*\*\*\*\*\*\*\*\*\*\*\*\*\*\*\*\*\*\*\*\*\*\*\*\*\*\*

Mother Astoria arrived on a Saturday amidst some pomp and circumstance and was met by a group of gawkers and a reception committee of sorts, consisting mostly of older women who hung on her every word. She was immediately embroiled with Brother Daniel Lee and some of his flock who had shown up for her arrival. They loudly proclaimed that the devil's own sorceress had arrived amid our fair town. When pressed, Brother Jamison later stated that he loved Mother Astoria but like Paul and his buddies in the New Testament, he was merely condemning the sin of fortune-telling. After being ushered away from Brother Jamison and his flock of demon-chasers, Ms. Temperin was taken to the Wagon Wheel Motel to secure a cabin and freshen up a bit before getting down to the serious work of divining the location of Johnny Blue.

# Chapter 4

Every Friday evening finished another work week at Meramec Ice and Fuel. In 1956 Dad didn't work with either ice or fuel. He drove an Anheuser Busch beer truck and made deliveries to taverns and package stores in Crawford and Phelps counties in Missouri.

When it became obvious that the grade A dairy farm at Jake's Prairie was never going to be anything more than a break-even proposition, Dad applied for, and got a job with Meramec Ice and Fuel as a bottled gas delivery driver. He did so well at that job he was asked if he would like to drive an Anheuser Busch beer delivery truck. He answered in the affirmative and was promoted to delivering beer which paid better.

Dad and Mom had a long indirect association with Meramec Ice and Fuel because they brought their freshly butchered beef and pork into Dogwood and stored the meat in their frozen storage locker in the locker plant. The concept was much like a person with money storing cash in a bank safety deposit box. We didn't have the money for our personal freezer so my parents paid a monthly frozen locker fee and put their goods which needed to be frozen in there and were given a key so they could access the food when they came into town.

Life on the farm had been difficult for both Dad and Mom. They arose around 4 AM and began milking around thirty head of Holstein and Jersey milk cows, by hand during the early years of the dairy. Later they used individual Surge milking machines which hung over the cow's back by a strap with four suction cups which were attached to the four teats on the cow's udder. This process was much better than hand milking but still required taking the Surge milk container to the cooler after milking every couple of cows. The raw milk was poured into ten-gallon milk cans which were kept cold in a circulating water cooler. The milk would be stored in these cans until the milk truck would come by every other day, pick up the full cans, and leave the same number of empty cans which had been cleaned and sterilized.

After the milking was completed, Mom would fix a quick breakfast and then drive to Owensville where she would work all day in a shoe factory. Her function was to oversee the "lasting" of the shoes, a job she had performed for Meeker Shoe Company in Joplin, Missouri, before she and Dad bought the 160-acre farm in Crawford County,

27

Missouri, and went into the dairy business. Mom later transferred to Dogwood Shoe Company and worked there until she was old enough to retire and then filed for social security.

After breakfast Dad would go to the barn and clean the stalls, wash and rinse out the milk house and turn the cows out of the holding pen. The cows spent the day nibbling on grass and leaving lots of fertilizer piles in the fields. After cleaning the milkhouse, Dad would plow, cut brush, fix fences, or any of dozens of other tasks that would command his days on a small farm.

Mom would get home around 5 PM and the milking process would begin again. After which Mom would fix supper and we would listen to the old upright Motorola radio broadcast The Great Gildersleeve, The Lone Ranger, The Green Hornet, or perhaps a Browns/Cardinals game. We would all retire around 9 PM and begin the same process all over the next morning, seven days a week, 365 days of the year. During the Monday through Friday routine, Ken and I would walk to High Point school and attend classes at the knee of Ivan Spurgeon. There were kids from the first through the eighth grade in the one-room school. We didn't learn much: but if you were going to be a farmer, you didn't need to know much.

I never overcame the lack of mathematics offered at the little one-room school but my brother, who was three years behind me, did great. He went on to college, worked for Westinghouse, and became a Senior Fellow with the engineering firm.

Once in a great while Dad would take Ken and me to Brush Creek or the Meramec River to fish, a sport my father dearly loved. Once we even went to Rolla and watched the new John Wayne movie "Red River." But normally it was just work for my parents with two small boys left to amuse themselves exploring the hills and hollers or playing cowboys and Indians.

Life got better or worse, depending on one's perspective, after Dad and Mom sold the farm and we bought our home on Maple Shade Road in the thriving metropolis of Dogwood. Both Dad and Mom had fixed hours and steady incomes and the family now had the weekends free: well, free unless Dad had a bowling tournament somewhere.

About once a month during the summer, Dad would get me out of bed around 3 AM and we would begin our adventure to Bull Shoals Lake on the Missouri/Arkansas border for a day of bass fishing. Bull Shoals Lake covers 45,000 acres and has almost 1,000 miles of shoreline. There are hundreds of arms and coves which made for fantastic fishing in the 1950s. I think it was my Dad's goal was to fish every cove on the Missouri side of the lake. Bull Shoals was about 150 miles from Dogwood, and we would leave about 3:15 AM. When we got to Branson, Missouri, sometime around 6:30 AM, we would eat breakfast at the Branson Café. The Branson Café had been built in 1910 and was the only place in Branson to eat at the time. Branson was to become a tourist venue but in the 1950s it was a sleepy little town with one café, one small motel, and a filling station. And it was the biggest place between Route 66 and Bull Shoals Lake. Stopping at the café was a ritual of every trip to the lake and high on the priority list for a growing twelve- and one-half-year-old boy. My Dad's breakfast agenda was simple: order fast, eat fast, and let's get to the lake.

We would typically get our Arkansas Traveler boat and West Bend motor into the water around 7 AM and fish the entire day. Rarely would we load the boat for the return trip to Dogwood before dark thirty. Most of the time we would be cleaning fish with the darkness being illuminated by the headlights of Dad's vehicle. Dad would let me sleep all the way back home, unless he got sleepy and needed me to talk to, and when we got home, I immediately went to bed.

I enjoyed fishing but in shorter lengths than the twenty-one-hour excursions to Bull Shoals Lake. To my Dad, whining was not tolerated. No matter how tired my butt got on the aluminum boat seat or how much it itched after a rain shower, there was to be no complaining. We, or at least Dad, were having fun and no one could rain on his parade. We would normally have a bologna and cheese sandwich for lunch and then Dad would often have a mid-afternoon snack of bait shrimp or limburger cheese on crackers. I tended to lean more towards a Baby Ruth candy bar for a snack and never competed with him for the bait shrimp or horrible smelling cheese.

Some years later when I left home and went into the Air Force, my brother Ken became Dad's fishing companion, but I was the guy who was his angling buddy until I departed for the mysteries of the wild blue yonder. Summers were fun times, but the summer of 1956 was anything but fun…

# Chapter 5

Derwood (Woody) Rifel was born on November 3, 1932, the eldest child of Ruben and Mary Beth Rifel. Woody was born on a farm east of Dogwood and was just another normal kid who played basketball and softball while at Dogwood High School. He was bright and made good, if not great, grades in school. Woody was a good-looking young man with dark compelling eyes and black hair that curled around his ears no matter how much Brylcreem he worked into his locks. In Woody's case "a little dab" wouldn't do him any good at all. Woody was tall, standing about 6' 2" in his stocking feet and weighed about 200 pounds with no fat at all on his lean powerful body. Woody was the perfect specimen, the perfect all-American kid from the heartland of America, the guy the girls loved, and the boys were jealous of; then along came the Korean War.

■■■■■■■■■■■■■■■■■■■■■■■■■■■■■■■■■■■■

After all the smoke cleared following the end of WWII, Korea was divided into a communist North Korea and an anti-communist South Korea at a spot on the world map which intersected the two Koreas at a place called the 38th parallel. The communist North Korea was somewhat controlled by and got its marching orders from the old Union of Soviet Socialist Republics, Russia. The United States exerted essentially the same control and influence over South Korea. Immediately after the end of WWII the Soviet 25th Army was transported to North Korea and set up their headquarters at Pyongyang for a prolonged stay. The Soviet forces in the North and the American forces in the South were described as present in the respective countries to rebuild the infrastructure and military following WWII.

On March 12, 1947, then President Harry Truman delivered a speech which was to become known as the Truman Doctrine in which he promised that American troops would come to the aid of any country that was threatened by communism. On June 25, 1950, communist North Korea, supported by the Soviet bloc, invaded South Korea with 89,000 troops. The South Korean Army lacked the training or manpower to thwart the attack and the North Korean Army advanced all the way to Seoul in three days. On that same day, fearing that communist sympathizers would come to the aid of the invading army, South Korea President Syngman Rhee began what was to be referred to as the Summer of Terror and ordered the execution of more than 100,000 South Korean citizens. On June 27, 1950, President Harry Truman, true to his word, sent United States troops to Korea. The United States and other United Nations countries joined the war because they wanted to stop communism from spreading into South Korea. The fear was that if a "line in the sand" wasn't drawn and defended, communism could spread without serious opposition.

On the United States Independence Day, in 1950, the North Korean Army advanced on Osan. The American forces were composed of soldiers of the 21st Infantry of the 1st Battalion who were equipped with antiquated and ineffective weapons. The North Korean force was made up of the 16th and 18th Regiments of the 4th Infantry Division, backed up by the 105th Armored Regiment. The American side had 540 men and no armor piercing artillery. The United States Army quickly discovered that the little yellow men were a force to be reckoned with.

On the 5th of July, the American soldiers held the line for almost three hours against an overwhelming force. Though encircled by North Korean troops, most of the American soldiers were able to escape leaving the wounded behind in the care of a handful of medics. The wounded and the medics were later found buried in a shallow grave, their hands tied behind their backs, and shot in the head. All told the American task force lost about forty percent of its troops with twenty-one wounded, eighty-two captured and sixty confirmed dead. Almost all the dead had been executed by the North Koreans. The North Koreans lost four tanks, eighty-two wounded, and forty-two killed. The Americans had entered the fray thinking they would enjoy an easy victory over an upstart enemy. They left the battlefield realizing they were in for a protracted and gut-wrenching war.

The World War II Hero General Douglas MacArthur, who oversaw all Allied forces in the Southwest Pacific, was placed in charge of the military effort in Korea. MacArthur wanted to conduct a Marine amphibious landing at Inchon so that American troops could attack the North Koreans from Pusan and Inchon. But he couldn't get other military leaders onboard with the idea. Finally, MacArthur sold the plan at an August 23, 1950, meeting of United States military leaders at his headquarters in Tokyo, Japan. MacArthur received official go-ahead for the Inchon landing which was code-named Operation Chromite and the port was captured on September 15, 1950. American forces converged on the North Korean army from both the north and south, killing or capturing thousands of enemy soldiers.

Following MacArthur's success at Inchon, the conflict would evolve into a tit-for-tat operation with both the Americans and North Koreans taking and surrendering first one hill, valley, or village only to have the other side retake it within days.

\*\*\*\*\*\*\*\*\*\*\*\*\*\*\*\*\*\*\*\*\*\*\*\*\*\*\*\*\*\*\*\*\*\*\*\*\*\*\*\*

After graduation from high school, Woody went to work for the Meramec Mining Company in one of its mines near Meramec State Park between Sullivan and Pea Ridge, Missouri. The mine produced magnetite-iron ore and the mine was one of the better paying jobs in the area. Woody was a hard worker and had received one promotion and was in line for his second advancement when he started hearing rumors of a Korean War draft.

The Korean War draft, which exempted all World War II veterans, called up men between the ages of eighteen-and-a-half and thirty-five years of age for terms of duty averaging two years. In June of 1951, the Universal Military Training and Service Act was passed, requiring males between eighteen and twenty-six years of age to register.

One day when Woody was listening to KTTR radio, Rolla, Missouri, he just happened to hear a discussion concerning the Korean War Draft which the guest said would become law in just a few weeks. Woody was born in November of 1932 and was almost twenty when he decided to go ahead and volunteer. He knew he would get a draft notice in the much-touted upcoming draft that was to start after June 1951.

Woody went to the Marine Corps recruiting office in Rolla and enlisted in the United States Marine Corps; figuring if he had to go to Korea he might as well be with the best fighting men in the military. Woody quit his job at the mines and went back home for a few days and then back to Rolla where he boarded a bus along with other recruits to go to Jefferson Barracks in Saint Louis. At Jefferson Barracks he was processed, given a medical examination, and sworn into the Marine Corps. On the bus ride into Saint Louis several other young men were picked up at different little towns on the route. At Jefferson Barracks the recruits were given a comprehensive physical examination to include an eye test and color blindness test along with a brief psychological interview. At the end of the process Derwood (NMI)

Rifel and several other young men were sworn in as Marines; Woody was now a Marine recruit.

The young men were assigned cots and spent the night. After breakfast and some more processing, they were taken by bus to the railroad depot and placed on a train headed for the Marine Corps Recruit Depot at Paris Island, South Carolina. They were to be transformed from farm boys, street wise thugs, and bankers' sons, amongst others into killing machines.

The new recruits arrived at the Paris Island recruit depot late in the evening and their training began immediately as they were thrust into the stressful whirlwind of in-processing, getting their heads relieved of hair (some would say haircuts), issued uniforms and gear and undergoing more medical examinations. They got to bed in the early morning hours and were rousted out of their bunks well before sunrise to march to chow and start their training experience. Next on the agenda were strength tests and then written tests to evaluate their cognizant ability and determine if they were qualified for more specialized training. Then there was more processing and indoctrination before the fun really began with classes in military and marine history, hand-to-hand combat training, rifle marksmanship training, and confidence building drills; all of which were accompanied by endless harassment.

At the end of twelve weeks Woody was a Marine, a one-man fighting machine that was part of a large and lethal organization whose sole purpose was to kill other human beings. After finishing basic recruit training, Derwood (NMI) Rifel was assigned to the 1st Marine Division and shipped out to Marine Corps Base, Camp Pendleton, California. Woody was now a part of the "Old Breed."

*************************************

Early November 1951 found Derwood (NMI) Rifel in South Korea compliments of a free ride across the ocean from San Diego, California, to Korea on the USS Noble. The USS Noble was anything but. The sleeping berths were hot, crowded and miserable. No one wanted to go down into the bowels of the ship to sleep because it consisted of narrow canvas cots hinged to the wall and stacked six high, with maybe two feet separating one bunk from the one above. When the sea was calm enough so that there wasn't saltwater spraying over the decks, Woody and his friends slept on the deck separated from the steel surface by their ponchos. During the sixteen days at sea there was nothing to do but lineup for breakfast, eat, leave the chow hall and then get back in line for lunch and repeat the process for supper.

The seas were heavy at times and several of the guys lost their breakfast or one of the other two meals while standing in line. Sometimes the seasick marines would make it to the rail and decorate the ocean and sometimes they splattered the deck and their friends. As they got closer to Korea the temperature started to fall. They huddled like sardines below deck to try to escape the cold temperature and bone chilling salt spray. The showers sprayed saltwater and the Navy provided them with special soap which was supposed to lather but acted as a defoliant and took off the first layer of skin. After sixteen miserable days they arrived at Pusan Harbor, Korea.

The marines were taken ashore in tenders and walked into an enormous maze of a tent city adjacent to a soccer field/stadium. There were telephone poles with loudspeakers mounted on them at locations scattered around the stadium. The new arrivals milled around most all day listening for their name to be called with instructions on where to go and which truck convoy to report to for transportation to their new duty station. Woody's rifle platoon was assigned to the far western end of the United Nations outpost defending a thirty-five-mile line that encompassed the Pyongyang to Seoul corridor. Welcome to the outpost war.

*************************************

From 1952 until the end of the war in 1953, the term "Outpost War" was used to describe the skirmishes revolving around the holding, losing, and retaking of various combat outposts along this key piece of terrain. This all changed in March of 1953 when the Chinese launched a massive offensive across the United Nations line killing many Army and Marine defenders and altered Woody's life forever. There were 4,004 dead Marines and 25,864 more wounded during the Korean War. Some were wounded in more ways than one…

# Chapter 6

Years after we left the farm my mind would often wander to the serenity and beauty of the place. Yes, there was little in the way of attraction beyond hard work and the scraping of a meager living from the soil and a few milk cows. But as I have grown older there has always been a yearning to return to the simple life, the freedom from stress, and the beauty of the old home place. In my mind's eye I would sit on the side of the hill behind the house and peer at the dogwoods ablaze in their glory displaying large greenish-white blooms intermixed with the occasional tree with pink blossoms. The dogwood is such a popular and beautiful tree in Missouri that it was named the state arboreal emblem (state tree) in 1955.

Chicory, a type of grass that displays odorless blue blooms which glistens in the sunlight and makes September seem to be a little bit of heaven, grew on the hillside across the creek where Dad had cut some trees for firewood. Some folks dig up chicory and, after drying and grinding it into a powder, used the root to add flavor to coffee. Spring would bless the same hillside with horsemint, a white flower with green in the center. Then starting in May through the remainder of the summer, ironweed and morning glory would blend in a canopy of color. Ironweed has white flowers with green centers and morning glory has soft blue trumpet-shaped blossoms and interesting three-lobed, pointed leaves. Walt Whitman was so taken with the morning glory's blossoms that he said, "A morning glory at my window satisfies me more than the metaphysics of books."

As my mind's eye would walk alongside the small spring-fed creek which flowed through our farm, I could see the old swimming hole where Ken and I swam. Upstream towards the springhead are the limestone hillsides that we played on and once caught a groundhog and put him into a cage to impress our Dad. Beyond the limestone dotted hillside was the old cemetery. We would explore the graveyard and check out the mounds in the woods in search of arrowheads. Near the cemetery stood the blackberry vines where my mother would take Ken and me while she was filling her basket with berries and fending off the occasional black snake which infested the area.

Across the field from the blackberry patch was Brush Creek which ran along the back side of the farm. The creek was lined with Sycamore trees and the occasional persimmon tree. We would fish along the creek. When we were going to the Osage

River or some other larger stream, we would seine minnows out of the creek for bait for our fishing expeditions. Once when the creek had been swollen by rain and then receded Dad and my brother-in-law, Jim Blunt, caught a twenty-pound catfish while seining. Dad took the fish to town in a large tub and showed the fish to everyone he saw. Never known for telling the truth when it came to fishing, Dad told them he had caught it on a red worm using a cane pole.

Returning on the east side of the farm were fields which Dad planted in permanent pasture for the cattle. The spring fed creek curved and followed the side of a hill until it exited our property. Down the hill next to our barn was the baseball field I would roam with Dad hitting me fly balls. I would catch the ball and then throw it to Ken who would relay it back to Dad. The barn sat on top of a gentle incline from the field and had a wagon road which led down the hill and into a rutted lane with barbwire fences on both sides. I got a Western Flyer bicycle for my tenth birthday and took off down the hill picking up speed but couldn't stop the machine, got flipped by a rut, and got initiated with the barbs on the fence. My mother cleaned the blood off me and wiped my cuts with turpentine to keep them from festering. Not my most fun day!

Many are the hours that I have daydreamed about the farm and can still see the old farmhouse and barn in my mind's eye. The farmhouse was the worst of the place. It had clay floors on the ground level and little spaces where the moon and stars would peek through on the second floor. The smokehouse and root cellar were the only structures which were still standing when I last visited the farm several years ago. Remembering the tranquility of the lifestyle on the farm has given me hours of relaxation during the years since we moved away from that simple existence. Daydreaming about what no longer exists isn't anything more than a temporary escape, but it beats Valium or Xanax without the possibility of side-effects. Sadly, the realities of life's trials and tribulations are always waiting when we return to the present.

It is said that you can never go home, but as I advance in years, I find myself returning to the childhood farm more and more often. Perhaps we seek serenity and an escape from a maddening world as we reach the last few chapters of our lives.

\*\*\*\*\*\*\*\*\*\*\*\*\*\*\*\*\*\*\*\*\*\*\*\*\*\*\*\*\*\*\*\*\*\*\*\*\*\*\*\*

In 1954 Dad and Mom sold the farm including implements and livestock to Rod

Freeze for the sum of $5,000.00. After taking possession of the place, Mr. Freeze boarded up the windows on the house, removed the roof, and used it for a corn crib.

After moving into the big town of Dogwood, Ken and I spent much of our summers walking from our home on Maple Shade Road out county road PP to Lick Creek and explored the limestone caves dotting the hillside along the banks of the stream. Some of the caves were large enough we could stand upright in them and some we had to crawl on our stomach to get more than a couple feet into the underground tunnel. Sometimes these tunnels opened into a room large enough to sit or stand in and sometimes we would have to wiggle back out of the tunnel when we came to a dead end. Other times I, being in the lead, would see some eyes back in the crawlspace peering back as the beam of my flashlight explored the tunnel ahead. We would then start backing out of the hole! It never occurred to us that limestone was soft and fragile and could have broken at any moment and trapped us inside one of the openings. Kids tend not to consider the possible implications of their actions and proceed on impulse. Luckily, we were never hurt beyond the expected scratches and bruises associated with crawling into the openings.

My parents are long dead so I can now reveal how stupid Ken and I were as kids. They probably knew and just never discussed having given life to idiots.

Having explored most all the caves that we found along Lick Creek; we turned our attention to the caves along the Meramec River we had discovered during our swimming expeditions. When all those underground exploring opportunities along the creek and river were extinguished, we turned our attention to exploring the storm drain system which ran under the town of Dogwood. Most of the drains pretty much followed Franklin and Main Streets with a few arms branching off on Spencer and Smith Streets.

The drainage system had been put in place when the town of Dogwood was being developed in the early 1900s, long after the town was platted in 1857. The drainage tunnel system was large enough we could walk upright and was perhaps three or four feet wide in most places. It was a great place to make believe we were in the trenches and underground tunnels of France during WWI. The drainage system was reasonably safe, and we had only to watch for the possibility of a water snake or some other critter who called the tunnels their home. There was always an abundance of rats which scurried off as we approached them.

# Chapter 7

Sycamore was a short street which branched off Maple Shade Road in Dogwood and in the 1950s there were only a couple houses on the street. There was a single-story house with a partial basement on the street that law enforcement would later discover had been rented by a man using the fictitious name of Windsor Michael Johnson. The driver's license the man had used as identification was a forgery and gave his address as 1013 107th Street, Overland, Kansas. Investigators would later discover the address was to a vacant lot. The man paid a month's lease and security deposit with cash which left no hint to his identity. His car was a dark green Studebaker with Kansas plates, or so the owner John Markel remembered though he couldn't be entirely sure.

John and Mary Markel had built the small house in 1951 when John returned home from the Korean conflict. He had received a medical discharge based on a training injury received during his tenure in the army. Shortly after the house was completed and they moved in, Mary was stricken with cervical cancer. After a short bout with the disease, she died in the summer of 1952 at thirty-two years of age. John had

Mary's body taken to Malden, Missouri, where she was buried in a family plot. John was devastated and just couldn't continue to live in the house. After removing some personal effects, he rented it out from time to time when he had opportunity.

When the house was rented for the one month to Mr. Johnson it was sparsely furnished and had become somewhat run down from lack of upkeep and maintenance. The Masonite siding had mildewed, and the paint had peeled in several places. The yard was grown up with tall grass and weeds. John just didn't have the funds to pay someone to keep the yard mowed.

John had listed the house for sale with Dogwood Realty a couple of times but never got an offer he found enough to recover the construction cost.

John had taken a job in West Plains, Missouri, working in a foundry and only came back to Dogwood when he was required to do so to sign papers to rent out the house. When the Dogwood Realty had called him, he had almost refused to drive to Dogwood when he was told that it was only going to be a one-month rental. But he was curious regarding the tenant, the condition of the house, and needed the money. So, he drove North on Highway 63 to Licking and then got on Highway 19 to Dogwood. After stopping by the Midway Restaurant for a sandwich, he met Mr. Johnson at the house at 2 PM.

\*\*\*\*\*\*\*\*\*\*\*\*\*\*\*\*\*\*\*\*\*\*\*\*\*\*\*\*\*\*\*\*\*\*\*\*\*\*

When Johnny Blue walked up Main Street, he saw Ms. Margaret Shuler watering her geraniums and waved to her. Ms. Shuler was a maiden lady who lived with her elderly mother in a suite in the hotel. Her father had died some years previously and had left the hotel to her with the proviso that she would care for her mother and provide her with a home. Ms. Margaret was as good as her word and cared for her mother until she died. Ms. Margaret had entertained a few suitors through the years, but none struck her fancy, so she decided to just stay single. As she grew older, she relished her decision not to marry. She saw many a woman being tied down with having to take care of some old coot who was either ill and required constant care, or lazy and unable or unwilling to provide a decent living. She had the hotel and a steady income from lodgers. She was satisfied with her lot in life.

As one went north on Main Street it became Route 66 right after you passed the Wagon Wheel Motel. The Wagon Wheel Motel had been a thriving business when

Route 66 welcomed thousands of travelers who were either headed to or from Saint Louis. After the new I-44 was completed the Wagon Wheel Motel went the way of hundreds of other motels, restaurants, and cafes. Some businesses simply closed shop and others reinvented themselves as some new type of business.

Years later there would be a revitalization of Route 66 and thousands of vacationers would drive east or west on the portions of the old highway that were open to traffic. Cafes and other attractions were refurbished and welcomed diners, gawkers, and even a few motel guests. The Wagon Wheel Motel was among those that were refurbished and turned into a motel and gift shop. The big attraction for tourists who later would come to Dogwood was to see the murals that were painted on the buildings along old Route 66 in the center of town. Fifty years after Route 66 was closed, old businesses would sell monogrammed coffee cups, small magnetic Route 66 signs, and a wide range of Chinese goods which the pilgrims couldn't get enough of.

\*\*\*\*\*\*\*\*\*\*\*\*\*\*\*\*\*\*\*\*\*\*\*\*\*\*\*\*\*\*\*\*\*\*\*\*\*\*\*\*

Jack and Betty Lambert bought their home at 117 Chestnut Lane in Dogwood,

Missouri, during the spring of 1953 and lived there with their children, a couple dogs and one long haired cat. Jack worked at Meramec Caverns as a tour guide during the summer months and cut and sold firewood to augment that income in the winter. Betty worked as a teller at Dogwood State Bank on Main Street. They only had one automobile, a 1950 Chevrolet pickup truck that Jack drove to work at Meramec Caverns and then used it to haul wood in the winter. Betty caught a ride to work every day with Maude Harris, a lady who worked at Hayes Shoe store just up Main Street from the bank. Between their joint incomes the Lamberts provided a home and the necessities for themselves and their children.

After Johnny Blue waved to Ms. Shuler he continued north on Main Street until it transitioned into Route 66. From there he cut across a small field to get on Fletcher Road which intersected with Chestnut Lane. As he crossed the field, he tried to catch a cricket or two and jumped a rabbit which bounded off and then hid in a small brush pile. Since it wasn't quite dark Johnny Blue decided to walk up Sycamore Street and look at all the dogwood trees that lined the street and dotted the bare lots and the house that had several dogwoods in the yard.

Like most kids in Middle America in the 1950s, Johnny Blue could wander around Dogwood. But if he didn't get home before it got dark his mother would worry, and his dad would make sure his hind end paid the price for his tardiness and for upsetting his mother. Johnny Blue had miscalculated the time before dark and cut across a yard to go to his house by the back way. He noticed a light on in the cellar as he walked by the house. Being by nature a curious kid he stopped and looked in the basement window. What he saw scared him to death and caused him to wet his pants and run.

# Chapter 8

After a large breakfast at Midway Restaurant Mother Astoria engaged in conversations with everyone at adjoining tables and handed out business cards. In addition, she informed onlookers that she would be at the Wagon Wheel Motel if they needed their fortune told. After canvassing the large dining room, she left by the side entrance and began looking for Doc Jones's city marshal car. Doc had told her that he would meet her alongside the Franklin Street door at 9 AM sharp. As Mother Astoria looked north on Franklin Street, she spied no Doc Jones and looking around she saw only the intersection of Route 66 (Main Street) and Highway 19 (Franklin Street) and a few automobiles parked alongside Franklin.

Mother Astoria had asked Doc Jones to secure some piece of clothing from the Lamberts that Johnny Blue had worn recently. Since she was hung up waiting for Doc Jones, she decided to walk across Main Street and hand out some business cards at the service station to a couple men who were waiting for their gas to be pumped. Then she crossed Franklin Street and went into Meramec Ice and Fuel, handed out more cards, then went into the IGA Foodliner and did the same thing. Even if she didn't have any success finding the missing boy, she might at least do a little fortunetelling business while she was in this town! The world was full of rubes and they had always provided her with a decent income from foretelling a future that could apply to most anyone.

Finally, about 9:30 AM Doc Jones showed up with a little shirt Johnny Blue had worn to a little league baseball practice just a few days prior to his disappearance. Mother Astoria took the shirt and walked around for a few minutes as if in a trance and then began walking up Main Street toward the middle of town. After she got to the corner of Smith and Main Streets, she turned on South Smith Street and walked by Hayes Shoe Store. She slowly walked on to the end of the street and Hiney Swint's pool hall. She then walked across South Smith Street to the front entrance of a rather low-class pool hall and bar and began walking north. She stopped when she got to the 5 & 10 cent store and went inside.

By the time Mother Astoria arrived at the 5 & 10 she had acquired a large following of onlookers. She went inside the 5 & 10 and walked the isles, stopped and said offhand "I can feel the child's presence in this place." Mother Astoria was on safe ground with her statement because there probably wasn't a kid in Dogwood who hadn't been in the 5 & 10 to buy gum or candy at one time or another. In fact, when I was in the 5th grade I left the school grounds at lunch and went to the 5 & 10 which was about two blocks from school and stole a couple pieces of candy. I had scarcely gotten reseated after the lunch break when my Dad appeared at the classroom door, came in, and spoke in hushed tones with my teacher, Mrs. Nuddleman. Mrs. Nuddleman called me up to the front of the class and stepped aside. My Dad asked me to bend over her desk and proceeded to use his trouser belt to teach me the error of my ways. Larceny was not to be tolerated in the Shuey family and I haven't stolen so much as a paper clip since the reckoning.

Mother Astoria then left the 5 & 10, walked on down Smith Street and went through the underpass which had been built to allow school kids to walk under Route 66 thereby keeping them safe. The underpass was used to avoid getting run over by some idiot who hadn't slowed down as he came into Dogwood. Once Mother Astoria was through the underpass, she made a left and started towards the Robert Judson Hardware and Lumber store. As she walked by the Methodist Church she stopped and stood there as if considering something of great importance. She then turned up the sidewalk to the church and opened the front door leading into the sanctuary; churches were unlocked in the 1950s and anyone could walk in at any time. Mother Astoria claimed that she could feel Johnny Blue's presence in the church. In fact, she had a 50/50 chance of being correct because there were just the Methodist and Baptist Churches in the middle part of Dogwood. Well, there was the Catholic Church on the other side of the school, but I guess she didn't consider it or, more likely, didn't know it was there. Anyway, she hit on the right church because the Lamberts attended the Methodist Church. Brother Daniel Lee Jamison would later contend that someone had let the cat out of the bag regarding where the Lamberts attended church and the clairvoyant had used the information to hoodwink the onlookers.

After leaving the church Mother Astoria started walking back down Main Street holding on to the baseball practice shirt like it was a sacred vestige. She stopped every few feet and stood still as if she were listening to a distant voice that only she could hear. After pausing to allow some divine revelation, she would then start walking again. When she got close to the intersection of Main and Franklin Streets, she stopped and knelt as if she were praying. She began shaking as if she were having a seizure or something. When she lifted her head, her eyes were rolled back so that only the whites shown. She broke out in a sweat and large beads of perspiration started forming on her face as if she were suddenly taken with a high fever.

Mother Astoria proclaimed, "He's here, I can feel him here!" The problem was that there was no "here" here. She was just standing in front of a small service station and the closest building of any size was the Midway Restaurant on the far side of Franklin Street. The Meramec Ice and Fuel was on the other side of Main Street as were two other small filling stations on either side of Franklin Street. She continued to insist that she could feel the presence of Johnny Blue. Mother Astoria was obviously shaken, as if she had received some message that even she didn't anticipate or understand. She was in Dogwood to fleece the country bumpkins, not to be scared by her own act.

Doc Jones was less than convinced but he called Sheriff Dills who arrived within the hour with a couple of deputies. The sheriff and his deputies looked in every nook and cranny of the service stations and then did a room by room search of the Midway Restaurant and offices on the second floor. Other than upsetting some tenants and disrupting the kitchen staff, they found nothing of interest. They then turned their attention to the Meramec Ice and Fuel Company and looked in every room and still found nothing. They didn't look in any of the frozen food lockers because that would require calling in every renter in order to gain access to each individual frozen food locker.

At about this point Brother Jamison asserted himself into the proceedings and proclaimed again that Mother Astoria was of Satan and she knew nothing regarding the disappearance of Johnny Blue or his current whereabouts. The small crowd began to murmur and broke up and started drifting away to have coffee at the Midway Restaurant and discuss the day's events. Doc Jones and Sheriff Dills just shook their heads in wonder. The woman had seemed so convinced she was right, but they had found nothing at all to confirm that the child was or had been in any of the places they searched.

Mother Astoria stayed overnight and had a few folks drop by the Wagon Wheel to have their fortunes told. She met some of the committee members the next morning. They thanked her for coming and paid her the fee as promised. Everyone seemed to think that it was more money tossed down the drain!

As for Mother Astoria, she had felt something she had never experienced before.

She couldn't explain the sensation, but it had frightened her to her core. The boy was near the place she had received the revelation, she was sure of that.

# Chapter 9

Summer was an interesting time for the Shuey boys. Since Dad and Mom worked all day Monday through Friday, Ken and I were kind of on our own so to speak. Ken was my responsibility to watch over and make sure he didn't get into trouble. The problem was there was no one to watch over me and keep me out of trouble. I was twelve and one-half and Ken was nine and one-half. We were certainly not old enough to be left on our own for around twelve hours each day, but we were. In today's world our parents would be charged with child endangerment or some such thing. But it was the 1950s and a different world regarding conventional wisdom on child rearing. Being left alone for hours at a time might challenge the sentimentalities of some but it helped us learn to be self-reliant; a human trait sorely missing in today's world.

In 1956 kids often went barefoot during the summer. After about two weeks your feet got tough and you could walk on anything but hot black asphalt which got hotter than Hades. Parents let their kids wander around; it was just normal. Today letting kids roam around on their own for more than fifteen minutes would be considered a hate crime and law enforcement and Child Protective Services would show up on your doorstep to haul the parents off to some gulag. We didn't know we needed protection and I suspect for the most part we didn't.

On one horrible day Ken and I were kind of wandering around in Dogwood and decided to do some squirrel hunting. We took Dad's old Remington .22 rifle, a pocket full of shells, and headed out Highway PP towards Lick Creek. We went into the woods and walked down a dry creek bed in search of tree rodents.

We learned our technique for squirrel hunting from our father. One person would walk ahead, make noise, and shake brush. The other person would trail behind and watch for the squirrel to run around the tree and expose himself to the person with the rifle.

Everything went well for an hour or so and Ken and I changed positions a couple of times but hadn't seen any squirrels. We were taught to carry our rifle either over our shoulder or in the crook of our arm. In case the firearm discharged by some quirk, the bullet would go into the air or ground. I was about fifty feet ahead of Ken and shaking a bush when I heard a shot. I looked up in the trees to see a squirrel fall. But there was no

63

squirrel and when I turned to Ken he was on the ground.

I ran over and Ken was lying on his back with a bullet wound on his chest. I bent down to try to talk to him but got no response. I did confirm he was breathing. I picked up the rifle and opened the chamber; it hadn't been fired. I looked around but saw no one.

Even though I doubted he could hear me, I told Ken that I would be right back and took off running down the creek bed and then up the hill to Highway PP. As I ran thirty or so yards down the creek bed, I saw a group of kids running through the woods. When I came out on the road there was a house across the road and perhaps 100 yards to my right; I later found out it was the Isaac home. I ran to the house and beat on the door until a woman came and asked me what I wanted. I explained that my brother had been shot and we needed to call Paul Shanklin to come and get him and transport him to a hospital. The woman ran to the phone and called Shanklin Funeral Home and told him what had happened. She then called Sheriff Dills and informed him of the shooting.

I started to leave to go back to Ken, but the woman told me sit on the porch and wait for Mr. Shanklin because he would have no idea of where to find us if I left. After what felt like hours Mr. Shanklin drove up and a sheriff car arrived at the same time. Mr. Shanklin and the deputy grabbed a gurney and followed me down through the woods to where Ken was lying on the rocks and gravel of the creek bed. They picked Ken up and put him on the gurney and strapped him down so that he wouldn't fall off as they ran with him through the woods with me leading the way.

Mr. Shanklin put the gurney with Ken on it into the ambulance and I was told to stay with the deputy. Mr. Shanklin said that he would notify my Dad and Mom and that the deputy would take me home after he asked me a few questions. I told him about the kids which was all that I knew about the incident. Obviously, my brother had been shot by one of the kids. The sheriff's department would later state that the kids were shooting at tin cans and a stray bullet had hit Ken. Since we hadn't heard any shooting, we always wondered about the reality of that claim.

A second deputy arrived and took me home. Mom showed up at our home and was frantic to say the least. Dad had been located by the secretary at Meramec Ice and Fuel and he arrived shortly after Mom. They both were asking me questions at one-hundred miles an hour for which I had no answers. We all jumped in our car and headed for Phelps County Hospital in Rolla, Missouri.

Ken had awakened during the trip to the hospital and had been placed in intensive care on arrival. The bullet had entered the left side of his chest, gone through his left lung, hit a rib and deflected, nicked his spine and exited his back. The hospital staff inserted a large needle between Ken's ribs to drain blood and fluid from his lung. They got him stabilized and started administering large doses of antibiotics to keep him from getting pneumonia. They kept him in intensive care overnight and then moved him to a room the next morning.

Within a week Ken was back at little league baseball practice and suffered no lasting effects of the bullet wound. Ken was very lucky. He could have gotten pneumonia, or the bullet could have been a fraction of an inch further towards his spine and would have permanently paralyzed him. Mr. Shanklin and the deputies credited my calm reaction and quick run through the woods to get help for saving Ken's life; I have always felt I was somehow responsible.

Sixty-two years after the shooting, the shooter has never been identified, and obviously no one was ever charged. The important thing is that Ken survived the incident!

\*\*\*\*\*\*\*\*\*\*\*\*\*\*\*\*\*\*\*\*\*\*\*\*\*\*\*\*\*\*\*\*\*\*\*\*\*\*\*

The secret to exploring storm drains is to stay out of them for several days after a large rain. Ken had fully recovered from his gunshot wound and he and I waited for a full three days after a summer shower to go through one of the exhausts of the storm drain system and into the tunnel complex. There was a grating covering the water exit site but over the years one of the hasps had rusted away. We were able to pull the grille work away from the wall sufficiently to squeeze in. Ken and I both had flashlights and we started down the first long tunnel and kept a good lookout for the possibility of a water moccasin which could have found its way into the wet, cool shaft.

We could sort of keep track of where we were by guesstimating how far we had walked, marking the branch tunnels we passed in our mind, and remembering each turn we had made. We had toured the tunnel system several times and we had no concern about getting lost. By our estimation we were close to the intersection of Main and Franklin Streets and judging by the automobile sounds we were confident of our location.

As the automobile sounds grew louder, light began filtering in through the drain slots on the side of the road. It wasn't as bright as direct sunlight but was better than the small flashlights and illuminated the entire tunnel area near us once our eyes adjusted to the dim light.

As we neared the manhole cover ladder the stench became almost unbearable. Lying up against the wall of the tunnel was something wrapped in a gray blanket. As we got closer, we could see rats scurrying away as we approached, and we now knew something very dead was wrapped in the blanket. The putrid smell got stronger and stronger as we approached the intersection and ladder. I had a stick which I always carried in our explorations in case we came upon a brave rat or other critter in a cave or the storm drain system. I pushed against the blanket with the stick. When the blanket fell away a small foot and shoe appeared.

Ken and I turned and hauled buggy out of the tunnel and ran all the way to the water exhaust grille, squeezed out, and kept running. We ran all the way back to Midway Restaurant and told one of the waitresses that we needed to use the phone to call Doc Jones. After explaining that we had found something horrible she called for us. Doc was eating lunch and said he would come as quick as he finished eating.

Doc Jones arrived within just a few minutes and burped several times while we told him what we had seen. He and a man we didn't know went to the manhole cover nearest the intersection and with some effort got it up on one side and slid it out of the way. Doc Jones shined his light down into the hole, held his nose, and started down the metal ladder which led to the bottom. In a couple minutes we could hear Doc losing his lunch. When he came out, he was white as snow.

Doc didn't say much because two kids were within earshot. But it was obvious he had found something horrible and it had to be Johnny Blue. Doc contacted Sheriff Dills who contacted the Missouri State Crime Laboratory who instructed them not to tamper with the body. They would send out an investigation team as soon as possible.

We heard through the rumor mill that the body was so badly chewed on by the rats that a positive identification was impossible without medical and dental records. After a couple days we heard that the body of Johnny Blue had been positively identified. Once it was conclusive that the body was that of Johnny Blue Lambert, Dogwood was inundated with state investigators who were intent on solving the crime.

Our parents were happy and somewhat proud that we had found the body, but they were equally unhappy that we had been in the storm drain and instructed us to stay out of it in the future.

# Chapter 10

During the early winter of 1952 Woody's platoon leader sent out a five-man patrol from the very center of a company position on the Jamestown Line in west-central Korea. The group was following the trace of an abandoned trench line which was used by the Chinese Communists or the Americans depending on who controlled that area at any given time. Suddenly a Chinese machine gun cut loose with a horrible rat-tat-tat as it sprayed bullets towards the patrol. The patrol leader was killed in the initial burst of machine gun fire and two more marines were wounded. The patrol was pinned down with no way to advance or withdraw. The Lance Corporal who was leading the patrol was almost cut in half by the machine gun fire. Woody was the senior Private First Class on the patrol and assumed leadership. After the machine gun fire subsided Woody considered his options and decided to send the marine who was only slightly wounded back to the staging area to report the ambush and get a relief patrol to come and get them. The chances of the young marine sneaking through the Chinese lines were slim but there seemed no other option. Without relief they were going to be killed or captured, and the

Chinese often killed prisoners. Later Woody was to discover that the young marine was killed by the Chinese.

The marine left to attempt to get to the staging area and notify the company commander. Woody was left with one marine who had been shot through the shoulder and was losing a lot of blood, a dead patrol leader, a very scared kid from a farm in Kansas, and himself. Woody used his first aid kit to apply a compress on the bullet wound to the marine's shoulder and gave him a shot of morphine. The three living marines hunkered down and tried to keep from freezing as the temperature was about -5° C or 23° F, chilly to say the least.

As the night went on it became more and more apparent that a recovery squad wasn't coming to save them and take them back to the base camp. Woody could hear people moving around in the darkness and knew it had to be the little yellow bastards who wished all the Americans out of Korea. Woody began dragging the wounded soldier slowly back down the trench line with the scared young marine crawling along bringing up the rear. After they had moved perhaps 100 yards, a machine gun from a second location cut loose ripping the trailing marine to shreds in a hail of bullets.

Now it was just Woody and a badly wounded marine against what seemed to be the entire Red Chinese Army. The wounded marine had been clutching his rifle when Woody began dragging him but now the firearm was nowhere to be found. It had obviously slipped out of the wounded marine's hand as he was being dragged. Woody kept slowly dragging the wounded soldier who was moaning with each tug on his uniform collar. After perhaps another 100 or yards, Woody came upon the body of the marine who had gone for help. He hadn't made it back to notify their base camp. He had been hacked to pieces probably with a bayonet.

In just a matter of seconds the Chinese soldiers were on him, stabbed the wounded marine repeatedly with their bayonets, and snatched the rifle out of Woody's hands. Suddenly everything went black. When he regained consciousness, he was bound hand and foot and was in some type of makeshift hut with a Chinese officer peering at him with beady dark eyes behind Mr. Peeper's type glasses.

Had Woody been captured by the North Koreans, he no doubt would have been killed on the spot or summarily executed with other American soldiers and buried in a mass grave. The Maoist Chinese treatment of

American POWs was normally humane and only centered on political education with brainwashing and brutal treatment being the exception. Unfortunately, Woody was captured by a mixed bag of North Koreans and Chinese Communists.

Woody was interrogated for hours day after day and was beaten with a cane rod when he refused to tell the Korean officer what he wanted to know. What could a private first class tell the interrogators they didn't already know? Privates were not normally involved in war planning exercises. They were sent to the front to catch the bullets. Woody kept telling them he didn't know anything, and they kept beating him. After each questioning and beating, Woody was thrown into a small hut by himself. The hut had no heat and with only a pot to use for bodily functions. For food he would receive a small bowl of dirty looking rice twice a day.

Not content with merely beating Woody, the Koreans decided to play a sadistic game with him and the other captured soldiers. The Korean officer pulled out a Nagant M1895 revolver from his holster and laid it on his desk. In a few minutes a black army soldier was brought in and shoved into a chair beside Woody. The Chinese officer whose name was Captain Huang merely looked on as the Korean named Major Oh removed all the cartridges from the revolver and then ceremonially put one shell back in the weapon, spun the cylinder, and handed the weapon to Woody, pointed at his head and made a pulling the trigger motion with his index finger. Woody was surrounded by Chinese soldiers holding automatic weapons. Some smiled, some laughed. And one winced, but it was either play the game or be shot then and there. He played.

Woody put the revolver to his head and pulled the trigger. The weapon clicked and he began to whimper. Major Oh took the revolver out of Woody's hand, spun the cylinder and handed it to the black soldier who at first refused to play the game. But when he was told to either play or get a bayonet through the throat he decided to play. He put the gun to his head and while sobbing and shaking pulled the trigger. The explosion of noise rocked the tiny hut and brain matter and blood splattered all over Woody. The metallic smell of blood was overwhelming.

During the next few months Major Oh would play this game three more times with Woody and each time he won. Or perhaps he lost because the toll on his sanity was devastating. Woody would later think it would have been better if one of the bullets had taken his life.

Woody and several other American soldiers were returned to the American lines by their captors on August 1, 1953, in a prisoner swap, just days after the war ended in a stalemate on July 27, 1953. The war was over for Woody, but the mental damage inflicted by his capture would follow him all his days.

Woody was taken to a field hospital for examination where his wounds were treated. He was fed some decent food for a couple days and then sent to the 343rd General Hospital at Camp Drew, north of Tokyo, Japan. The psychiatrists at Camp Drew diagnosed Woody as suffering from combat related trauma to include moderate schizophrenia and acute depression. Woody underwent weeks of cognitive behavioral therapy and was pronounced cured by Army psychiatrists.

Woody was mustered out of the marines and sent back to Missouri as a well man. The problem was Woody wasn't well and never would be. He was a danger to anyone and everyone who irritated him. Any minor thing could set him off. Woody should probably have been taken to the Missouri State Mental Facility in Farmington, Missouri. But for whatever reason he was given a pass on his behavior on many occasions; probably because of his Korean service.

Woody had started drinking excessively and was a frequent visitor to the Crawford County jail. When he was reasonably sober, he would work as a pulpwood worker or try to win some money shooting pool at Hoyt McCann's pool hall where he was a regular and frequent winner. Drunk or sober Woody was an excellent pool player! I worked in McCann's pool hall racking balls and when I played and won, I received ten cents for racking the balls for the next game. I learned early on not to play pool with Woody because I simply couldn't beat him, ever.

# Chapter 11

After receiving notification from Sheriff Dills regarding the body, the state crime lab sent two technicians, John Barnish and Melvin Gaines, and a forensic pathologist named Elmer Jorash, to Dogwood. They were to photograph the site where the body was discovered, dust for fingerprints, secure the remains of Johnny Blue, and transport the body, or what was left of it, to the state crime laboratory for an autopsy. They cordoned off the area around the manhole cover and the exhaust point which we used to go in and out of the storm drains. We thought all this was unnecessary because Ken and I, as far as we knew, were the only people who ever went in the storm sewers.

As it turned out, Mother Astoria was standing nearly over the remains of Johnny Blue when she was near the intersection of Franklin and Main Streets and received her epiphany. Some things are hard to rationally explain!

After the autopsy the crime lab established a presumed time of death based on the deterioration of the body, the type and life cycle of the bugs found feasting on the remaining tissue, and the decomposition of the internal organs. Their estimate wasn't very precise, but they theorized the remains of Johnny Blue had been in the water runoff tunnel for a least two weeks.

Two state investigators, Jonas Belweather and Sidney Whitfield had accompanied the crime scene group and stayed and interviewed the city utility folks in order to establish how the body got into the storm drainage system. The investigators theorized, based on the fact there had been a heavy summer shower a couple days prior, that the body had been dumped into one of the storm water run-off openings upstream from the site where the body was found and then moved by the flowing water until it hung up on the ladder and remained there until it was discovered. They supposed a person or persons unknown had stopped along Main Street right next to the street water inlet and slid the body through the opening. Since the opening was only thirty to forty feet from where Johnny Blue's body was found they thought that was a reasonable conclusion.

Next the investigators turned to Ken and me and began quizzing us. When they questioned me, I admitted I probably had seen the boy at school because the high school, middle school, and grade school were all in the same building complex and there weren't hundreds of students attending. I further explained I wouldn't have paid any real attention to him because he was in the fourth grade and I was in the eighth. Ken acknowledged he knew the boy slightly because he would see him during recess when the fourth and fifth graders were on the playground at the same time. But he hadn't known him well and not at all away from school. After repeating the questions and adding some completely silly ones numerous times and asking us about 10,000 times why we were in the storm drain, they let us go home.

The only clear fingerprints the forensic people found were those of Doc Jones which were left when he climbed down the manhole ladder. They did determine the cause of death was blunt force trauma; Johnny Blue had been hit on the head with a heavy object which caved in his skull and caused massive brain damage. Death was instantaneous which provided the family with a small measure of comfort.

The investigators had no idea where Johnny Blue had been killed, why, or who might have committed the horrible deed. The baffling thing was the investigators could find no motivation for anyone to kill Johnny Blue. He was just a little boy. Who and why was always the difficult part of an investigation when the person who committed the crime wasn't caught in the act or compelling evidence wasn't present. This killing was even more difficult because of the young age of the boy and the lack of any apparent motive.

# Chapter 12

After Johnny Blue's body was released by the crime lab, it was picked up by Paul Shanklin who owned Shanklin's Funeral Home. The body was prepared as best Shanklin could and placed in a moderately priced casket which was sealed so that the body couldn't be viewed. The body lay in state at Shanklin's Funeral Home for visitation with the family members.

The funeral was held late on a Saturday morning and was attended by a couple hundred people. It was amazing to see how people who didn't know or care about the Lamberts just a few days prior would put on their Sunday best frocks and attend Johnny Blue's funeral. The services were held at the United Methodist Church on Main Street. Then the hearse containing the remains, followed by the crowd, preceded to the Oak Hill Cemetery for burial where some of the Lamberts' ancestors were interred.

There were few dry eyes at either the church service or the graveside ceremony. No one could understand the senseless murder of this beautiful child. A few friends of the Lamberts went to their home and stayed for a while trying to comfort them. The remainder of the attendees returned to their own lives and the Lamberts would revert to obscurity after a few days.

The good citizens of Dogwood were worried because, unless some deranged individual just stopped in Dogwood and decided in his twisted mind to kill a random child, there was a killer within their midst. Most everyone was a suspect on some level. As the days went by people became more and more edgy. The town needed closure to know that their children and grandchildren were safe to walk the streets and play outside without fear.

Three days after the funeral, Mark Baker, a sixth-grade student, came running into the 5 & 10 screaming that there were two men who were trying to get him. Doc Jones was called and a state trooper who was at Midway Restaurant eating lunch was summoned. They found two men in a white pickup truck exactly where the boy said they were and both Doc Jones and the trooper approached the truck cautiously. It turned out the two men were railroad employees who had never been in Dogwood and had been repairing a defective railroad crossing bell. When they had finished that task, they saw the boy and were merely trying to get directions to someplace to eat from him. They thought the boy was crazy because he went running away screaming. Doc Jones gave them directions to the Dogwood café and the Midway Restaurant and bid them a good day.

Ms. Hazel Snyder, a maiden lady who lived on Moss Street, called Doc Jones around 8 PM one night screaming and claiming someone was trying to get in her back door to kill her. Doc came around in his cruiser and walked around the house with his sidearm drawn and a flashlight in his other hand. The culprit turned out to be the unlatched screen door on the porch which was banging due to frequent gusts of wind. Every old maid and widow in Dogwood were double and triple latching their doors and locking their windows and shuddering at every unknown sound. Such was the tension in the town of Dogwood.

# Chapter 13

A female state investigator named Alisha Johnson took an interest in the murder of Johnny Blue. She asked her supervisor if she could do some snooping around on the phone to see if there were any other missing or murdered boys within a couple hundred-mile radius that fit the profile of this killing. The supervisor told her to "go ahead," just don't ignore her other work.

Alisha's task was made somewhat easier by the new direct number dialing system, where callers made their own long-distance calls. This innovation was first introduced into the Bell System during a trial period in Englewood, New Jersey, in 1951 and was fairly well implemented across the country by the mid-1950s. Alisha still had to contact an operator, tell her the city, state, and specific entity she wished to call. The operator would manually determine the destination area code and the phone number from a printed list and provide the information to Alisha. Then Ms. Johnson could directly dial the number on her rotary dial phone. Slow, but certainly faster than the old system.

After a couple days of calling various sheriff departments, Alisha hadn't found a single report of a boy who had been abducted; but she did find something that was very interesting.

There had been three recent incidents of young girls being abducted and never found. The first, a ten-year-old named Charlotte Webber in Carbondale, Illinois, in May of 1955. The second girl named Juanita Stills, age eleven, was abducted in Arlington Heights, Illinois, in October of 1955, and the third, a ten-year-old, named Margaret Tuttle, was abducted in Kearney, Missouri, in June 1956.

Intensive investigations by the police departments in their areas hadn't produced an arrest in any of the three abductions. The only thing that was similar regarding the missing children was that in two of the cases, an individual had reported seeing a dark Chevrolet panel truck in the areas where two of the girls went missing. One of the witnesses thought the truck had Kansas plates but wasn't sure.

Beyond the possibility of a dark panel truck being in the area where two of the girls were abducted, there were no other clues. And since no license plate sighting was positive, this bit of speculation wasn't particularly helpful.

Alisha thought she had hit a dead end but requested the files anyway and kept them just in case another female child would be reported missing.

*************************************

       Charlotte Marie Webber was a pretty, petite blond girl who was in the fifth grade at Carbondale, Illinois, elementary school and a cheerleader at Pop Warner football games. She liked to ride her bike and play hopscotch on the sidewalk in front of her house. On the evening she went missing she had been with two other girls a couple streets over from her house playing skip-rope. After the girls stopped playing, Charlotte headed towards her home for supper but never showed up.

       Mrs. Webber became alarmed when Charlotte hadn't showed up before dark and called her friends' parents and was told their daughters were at home and had seen their friend head for home shortly after they finished playing. That would have been about fifteen minutes before sunset. Mrs. Webber called the Carbondale police department and the desk sergeant reassured her that her daughter had probably just stopped to visit with a friend and there was nothing to worry about. About 10 PM Mrs. Webber went to the police station and demanded they get off their duffs and try to find her child. The desk sergeant called and got an investigator to come and speak with Mrs. Webber. He sent a patrol car to search the neighborhood.

The investigator, a large man with thinning hair named Carl Dovert, talked to Mrs. Webber and asked if Mr. Webber could have taken the child. Mrs. Webber told him that she and her previous husband had been divorced for about three years. He worked at some farm implement dealership in Nebraska and had shown little interest in paying his child support or visiting their daughter. Mrs. Webber had tried to no avail to get her ex-husband to pay his child support. She couldn't afford a lawyer and getting the divorce court to enforce its child-support ruling in another state was impossible. The short of it was, no, Mr. Webber wouldn't come back to Illinois and kidnap his daughter. And, no, she didn't know anyone who would want to take her daughter. The maternal grandparents were dead, and her ex-husband's family was disinterested in the child.

The Carbondale police department started a house-to-house search in the early morning hours and, other than irritating several residents on Charlotte's presumed route home, they accomplished nothing. Mrs. Rudolph Snell did recall seeing a dark panel truck that she had never seen in the neighborhood before as she was allowing her

Pekinese Fu-fu to relieve herself. Other than that, one tid-bit of information, the police drew a complete blank.

Days turned into weeks, weeks into months, and the child was never heard from again.

\*\*\*\*\*\*\*\*\*\*\*\*\*\*\*\*\*\*\*\*\*\*\*\*\*\*\*\*\*\*\*\*\*\*\*\*\*\*

Juanita Mae Stills was a charming eleven-year-old girl who was the brightest child in her sixth-grade class. Juanita was introspective, studious, and even at her young age knew she wanted to be a veterinarian. Juanita was near-sighted and wore little turquoise colored glasses. She liked her brown hair cut shoulder length and favored blue jeans and shirts rather than dresses or skirts. Juanita was well liked by everyone even though she wasn't very outgoing.

The Reverend Joseph and Delores Stills had lived in Arlington Heights, Illinois, for five years, having been assigned as the new minister to the flock at the Broad Street Methodist Church. The Stills had two other children, a younger girl and an older boy. Everyone seemed to like the Stills and had no reason to believe they would harm their child in any way.

On the evening Juanita disappeared she had been walking the family dog, which was her evening responsibility, down to a small park to let Jodi relieve herself. She always carried a poop scoop and a small paper sack to gather the poo, place it in the little bag, and place it in a trash container. Juanita never came home from the park and Jodi was heard scratching at the front door of the Stills' home.

Reverend Stills immediately hurried to the park, but Juanita was nowhere to be found. He rushed back home and called the Arlington Heights police department which sent a patrol car that arrived within fifteen minutes. A second police car arrived and began driving up and down the streets in the immediate area while the patrolman in the first car asked the Stills questions which provided no useful information. No, they didn't think their daughter would go into a neighbor's home. No, she wouldn't turn Jodi loose to go visit a friend. No, Juanita hadn't been disciplined and had no reason to be upset. And no, they had no idea what could have happened.

After driving up and down the streets near the Stills' home the patrolmen began knocking on doors and asking if anyone had seen the child. Some of the neighbors knew the girl and some didn't but a couple had seen the little girl walking her dog towards the park. No one had seen her return, and no one remembered seeing anything unusual. No one had seen strangers, or any vehicle which seemed out of place. It was as if Juanita just fell off the earth or vanished into thin air. Juanita Stills was never seen again after the day of her disappearance.

\*\*\*\*\*\*\*\*\*\*\*\*\*\*\*\*\*\*\*\*\*\*\*\*\*\*\*\*\*\*\*\*\*\*\*\*\*\*\*\*

Margaret Lea Tuttle was a precocious red-headed, freckle faced little imp of a girl who was always involved in some type mischief. She was the child who was always playing tricks on the other kids in her fifth-grade class. Everyone loved Margaret because she was fun to be around.

John and Maude Tuttle were model citizens. John was an employee of the City of Kearney, Missouri, and supervised the utility department. Maude worked part-time at a local veterinarian clinic three days a week. Both maternal and paternal grandparents lived in a suburb of Chicago, Illinois, where both the Tuttles had grown up.

Margaret had been riding her bicycle with two other girls from her class in school and they all decided it was time to return to their respective homes before it got dark. The other two girls made it home without incident. When Margaret hadn't returned home thirty minutes after dark, Mrs. Tuttle called first one of Margaret's bicycle riding friends' home and then the other. The mothers of both children stated that their daughter had seen Margaret taking a shortcut through the new housing area but knew nothing beyond that. John Tuttle tore himself away from his newspaper and got into his car thinking he was wasting his time, Margaret would be home any minute.

John turned on the new street where the houses were being built and saw Margaret's Western Flyer girls' bike lying on its side near a driveway but there was no sign of Margaret. John called "Peggy" as loudly as he could several times but got no response. He put the bike in the trunk of his car and went home and immediately called the Kearney police department. The dispatcher sent out a police patrolman who questioned the Tuttles for a few minutes and then began driving around the neighborhood shining spotlights into yards. A second police car showed up and they pulled into the new street, got out and began a house-by-house search of all the new construction on the street. They found nothing other than some tools that had been left on one of the job sites.

The Tuttles were questioned extensively and denied knowledge of any information regarding their child's disappearance. None of the neighbors had seen Margaret since early afternoon. Mrs. Duncan, who lived one street over from the Tuttles, told the police that she had seen a dark panel truck slowly drive by on her street earlier that afternoon while she was working in her flower garden but thought little of it at the time. It was probably just some type of service truck anyway. The police followed the lead of the panel truck and found no one who had any type service vehicle or knew anything about a dark panel truck.

Margaret "Peggy" Tuttle was never heard of again.

# Chapter 14

Maurice (Mo) Rifel was the younger brother of Woody and was one strange individual. As a child he was playing with matches in a small storage building. He had taken the matches from the kitchen and was lighting them one by one. He accidentally caught the building on fire when a match ignited some gasoline which had seeped from an old rusted can onto the floor of the building. Mo got trapped in the building and was severely burned on the left side of his face and shoulder. Woody saw the smoke, rushed into the shed and pulled his little brother out of the burning building and saved him from being burned alive.

The fire scarred Mo both physically and psychologically. His school mates made fun of him because of his disfigurement and girls had no interest in him. As a child Mo was constantly in some type of trouble and prone to get into fights with the other kids. As an adult he resorted to the only thing he was good at, fighting.

During the 1950s barn fighting was a favorite pastime in rural Missouri. A fight would be scheduled for a Saturday night in a barn on some farm and word of mouth would advise folks as to the where and when. Bare knuckles' fighting was illegal, so formal advertising wasn't prudent. However, Sheriff Dills would occasionally show up in the audience. Two fighters would square off and the onlookers would wager on who was going to win.

Mo was about six feet tall and rawboned, a good fighter for his weight but not great and won his fair share of matches. Unfortunately, the beatings he took in winning and losing influenced his thought processing abilities and made him even more volatile. Mo became little more than a common drunk whose goal in life seemed to be to see how much Stag beer he could drink every day. When he was drinking, which was most of the time, he became even more belligerent and abusive than normal.

Mo had a horrible temper and an even bigger chip on his shoulder because of the scarring on his face and the way he was shunned. When inebriated, Mo had threatened to kill people just for the fun of it. No one really trusted Mo and put nothing past him, nothing.

# Chapter 15

Frederick Louis Hempstein (Freddie) was a giant of a man, perhaps six foot two inches tall and weighed probably 250 pounds. He finished the fourth grade only because there was no special education facility in the Dogwood school system in which to place him or any other local institution available. He was withdrawn from school in the fifth grade because he simply couldn't comprehend the class material and was becoming frustrated and disruptive. For the most part Freddie was harmless and didn't cause any trouble in school, but he was mildly retarded and had achieved his educational potential.

As an adult Freddie was a gentle giant and rode a large red Western Flyer bicycle around Dogwood and rarely bothered anyone unless and until teenage boys teased and played tricks on him. Then he would get angry and might throw whatever was handy at the boys. He worked menial jobs around town: raking leaves in yards, loading trash and debris for transport to the city dump, unloading cement bags for Robert Judson Lumber Yard, and washing the occasional automobile. Freddie was intelligent enough to know the value of money and knew about how much he should receive for some mundane job. He could also make change when needed.

Freddie lived with his mother in a rundown house on West Phillips Street. Mrs. Daisy Hempstein worked at the Dogwood shoe factory and made just enough money to feed her and Freddie and pay the small amount of rent and utilities each month. Freddie's father had left when it became apparent his son wasn't quite right and he hadn't been heard from for years. At times the challenge of dealing with Freddie was almost more than his mother could handle. She strove to persevere.

Freddie could become agitated when he was teased but no one could recall him ever hurting anyone. He had chased some teenage boys who were teasing him, but it was more a bluff than a serious intent to hurt them. He had about as much chance of catching them as a plow horse would of winning the Kentucky Derby. After the incident he would join the boys in a good laugh. For all practical purposes Freddie was just a fixture of Dogwood. People accepted him, smiled when meeting him, and for the most part just left him alone.

The possibility that Freddie had killed Johnny Blue never occurred to any of Dogwood's citizenry. However, the possibility didn't escape the attention of the state investigators.

# Chapter 16

Pete Stilwell was a Ne-er-do-well who worked odd jobs around Dogwood and the occasional construction job in different locations in Missouri when that type work was available. Pete was prone to get drunk and become rowdy and abusive like many tavern rats tend to do when they get a snoot full of beer and think they are mean.

Because of his obnoxious behavior and alcoholism, he was basically ignored by the good people of Dogwood. Other than the beer hall class, no one even knew who he was. In one of his drunken stupors Pete could do most anything and had wrecked all the old rusted out trucks he had owned.

Because of his violent tendencies when he was drunk, which was most of the time, even his bar friends kept him at arm's length. No one had ever thought of him as being a child killer. On the other hand, he was unpredictable. In one of his drunken stupors he might do anything and then not even remember the act the next morning.

Pete was a frequent visitor to the Dogwood city jail and the county jail as well. He didn't even seem to mind being locked up. The food wasn't bad, and it was a free place to sleep. Stilwell was one of those individuals whose lot in life improved when he was incarcerated.

# Chapter 17

Oliver Wendell (Ollie) Tweek was a retarded man who was born in Rosebud, Missouri, into a large family of Tweeks. Ollie was a below average kid mentally until a mule kicked him in the head while he was cleaning out the horse stalls on the Tweek farm. The blow was glancing but nonetheless it caused some additional brain damage. Young Ollie lay unconscious for several days until the swelling in his head abated. He was no doubt lucky to have lived through the incident.

Honestly the mule accident didn't add much to his retardation, but the blow to his skull did leave him with a severe speech impediment. Unless one listened carefully it was difficult to understand what he was trying to say. Ollie tended to stutter and get confused on the correct word to use. His school mates would constantly make fun of him. All of Ollie's brothers and sisters would look after him and try to protect him from the ridicule of people who used him for sport, but to no avail. Ollie became very withdrawn and wouldn't normally speak unless directly spoken to.

When Ollie turned eighteen, he went to the Army recruitment center in Rolla,

Missouri, and volunteered for the military at the start of the Korean War. They processed his application and sent him to Jefferson Barracks in Saint Louis where he was classified 1-N because of his speech problem. The military physicians felt Ollie would be a hindrance to his fellow soldiers during times of combat because they wouldn't be able to understand what he was saying. Somewhat dejected Ollie returned to the farm. When his father asked why he was turned down Ollie replied, "I guess they want talkers, not fighters." Ollie didn't pass the mental acuity testing either but that wasn't common knowledge outside the Tweek clan.

Ollie and I worked together putting up hay on the Wayne Branson farm at Jake's Prairie during 1955 and the Jim Stubbleford farm north of Dogwood during the same summer. We got the same payment for our work; one cent a bale for each bale loaded on the farm wagon and placed in the loft of the barn. Ollie and I worked well together even though I couldn't understand much of what he said. Dad hired Ollie to work on the farm when he needed extra help and if it didn't require talking, Ollie did fine.

Ollie had a knack for getting hurt in the most peculiar ways. When we were loading baled hay on the farm wagon on the Branson farm, he was bitten on the index finger by a rat snake which had been caught up by the baler. Normally a rat snake bite isn't harmful but for some reason Ollie's finger got infected. Doctor Snyder was fearful he was going to have to remove the digit. As it turned out the infection responded to penicillin and no further treatment was required. Ollie was hooking a team of mules up to a plow and one of them stepped on his foot and broke two toes. Another time Ollie and one of his brothers were fishing on the Gasconade River in an old wooden flat bottom boat. Ollie took off his brogan boots and dangled his feet in the water to cool them. Along came an alligator gar and mangled his big toe on his right foot to the extent that it had to be surgically removed.

Ollie occasionally worked on our farm helping Dad fix fences. One cold morning he showed up and immediately headed for the outhouse. When he came out, he was carrying his jacket which was covered with toilet waste. The Shueys, always known for our refinement, had a "two-holer" and Ollie had somehow managed to let his coat fall into the second hole. Dad asked him if he was going to wear the nasty coat.

Ollie responded, "No, Mr. Claude, I just wanted to get my lunch sandwich out of the pocket."

Ollie was working on the Rufus Diller farm and Mr. Diller came out to the barn and found Ollie and Millie, his rather homely sixteen-year-old daughter lying together on a pile of hay. Ollie kept saying he wasn't doing anything. They were just talking. Mr. Diller made a big deal of the incident and notified Sheriff Dills. The sheriff interviewed Ollie and made an official report. As Ollie and Millie were both fully clothed, there was no evidence Ollie had done anything to harm the girl, so no charges were filed. But he was now recorded in the system and his reputation was sullied by all the local gossip.

# Chapter 18

When Johnny Blue looked in the basement window he was horrified. A young red-headed girl perhaps ten or eleven years old, strapped to a table with tape over her mouth. There was a large man wearing a flowery shift who was hurting the little girl as the tears rolled down her cheeks. There was another man sitting in a chair across from the window reading some type of magazine. Just as the man finished hurting the little girl the other man looked up and saw Johnny Blue looking in through the window.

Johnny Blue took off running and the man ran up the stairs. Johnny Blue intended to go through the back yard and across the field to his home but in his hysteria ran into the back fence which stretched across the back of the yard. Johnny Blue turned and ran back across the yard but on the opposite side of the house and was grabbed by the man as he ran by the front porch. The man had some type of wrench in his hand and hit Johnny Blue crushing his skull and then pulled him up alongside the house where he would be hidden from the street if someone came along.

The two men discussed what to do with the little boy and considered their options. They didn't know the area well so if they dumped the body it might be found before they could leave town. They decided if the body was stuffed in the storm drain system in Dogwood he probably wouldn't be discovered for months if at all and that would give them time to get rid of any evidence and leave town. They wrapped the body in a blanket, waited until early morning, and put the corpse of the little boy in the Chevrolet panel truck. The owner of the truck slowly drove to the water inlet on Main Street, stopped and quickly shoved the body through the opening and drove away.

It had taken all of thirty seconds after the panel truck stopped before it was moving again.

# Chapter 19

The state investigators started their in-depth interviews of suspects with Derwood (Woody) Rifel. They questioned Woody about the murder of the little boy for more than seven hours without a break. Belweather would work on him for about an hour and then Whitfield would take over. They only allowed him to use the bathroom and get a drink of water during the marathon questioning. After the break they started again asking the very same questions hoping to detect some variation in his answers.

Woody had been interrogated many times by the Chinese and North Koreans and compared to them these guys were mere amateurs. The Chinese and North Koreans had beaten him with canes, slapped him around, and made him play Russian roulette. All these guys did was ask the same questions over and over and make some silly threats.

Their questions were easy to answer because Woody had absolutely no idea of what they were talking about. He had heard some scuttlebutt in McCann's pool hall about a child being missing but he knew nothing and really wasn't very interested. After surviving the Korean War not much of anything bothered him and a child being missing certainly wasn't on his list of concerns. He was surprised when the investigators told him the boy had been killed. In a small town like Dogwood a murder was a rarity. In fact, anything more serious than the theft of a chicken was an oddity.

After about twelve hours of asking the same questions and receiving the same answers over and over the state investigators decided whatever this guy's faults, he knew nothing about the killing of the child. Since the interrogators were more tired than Woody, they let him go. They couldn't understand how a man could stay so calm when faced with the accusations they had confronted him with. If they only knew!

# Chapter 20

The state investigators were informed by Sheriff Dills that there had been a complaint filed against Ollie Tweek for child molestation. The investigators went to the Tweek farm to pick up Oliver Wendell (Ollie) Tweek for questioning. The elder Mr. Tweek told the investigators that Ollie and his brother Homer were in Nebraska working on the hay harvest. Corn was the big cash crop in Nebraska and Iowa, but they had been hired to help with putting up the hay crop. They had left about two weeks prior and wouldn't be back for another couple weeks. No, Mr. Tweek didn't know exactly where they were staying because they moved from one farm to the next following the cutting, curing, and baling of the hay. He said both his sons were grown and wouldn't contact him while they were gone unless something important the family needed to know happened. No, he didn't have an address. He did provide the investigators with the name and address of the farmer who had hired them to make the trip to Nebraska.

The investigators contacted the Missouri Highway Patrol and requested they contact the Nebraska Highway Patrol and have them go to the John Haskins farm in

Gering, Nebraska, and confirm that Ollie Tweek was employed there and the date of his arrival. It took a couple days to work through all the state to state bureaucracy and get the Nebraska troopers to go out to the farm. When they finally found Haskins, he confirmed both Ollie and his brother were indeed working on the area farms and had been there for a couple weeks. They then sent for Ollie and Homer and verified their identity by checking their drivers' licenses. And since they were working seven days a week during the harvest season, there was no way Ollie could have gone to Missouri after supper, killed and disposed of a child, and returned in time the following morning to eat breakfast at daylight and then start work.

The Nebraska authorities notified the Missouri authorities of their findings and convinced that Oliver Wendell Tweek was not a viable suspect, they lined him off their list of possible murderers.

# Chapter 21

Next on the investigators list was Maurice (Mo) Rifel whom they had picked up at a dive near the old post office building where he had been sucking down Stag beers and playing pool for several hours. Once Mo's mind cleared enough to understand why he was being questioned, he cursed the interrogators and accused them of being stupid. He had no interest in bothering some little boy and had no idea of what they were talking about. As the interrogators put more and more pressure on Mo, he asked them to take him to the county jail so he could get something to eat and take a nap. His responses to their repeated questions indicated he didn't know anything about the abduction or murder. In fact, it became readily apparent Mo didn't know much of anything about anything at all.

During the questioning, Sheriff Dills pecked on the glass window of the interrogation room and Belweather came out of the room. Dills said, "You fellows are barking up the wrong tree with Maurice Rifel. He just got out of the county work camp a few days ago. He served thirty days for drunk and disorderly and destruction of private property.

Because of Mo's arrogance and nasty demeanor, Belweather and Whitfield wished they could find some reason to put him in state prison for about twenty years; but alas, they had no justifiable reason to hold him. They asked him where he wanted to go and he said, "I told you dumb asses to take me to the county jail in Steeleville. Are you deaf?"

They took him back to the beer joint and were exceedingly glad to be rid of him.

# Chapter 22

Last on the list for interrogation was Frederick Louis (Freddie) Hempstein. The investigators found Freddie riding his Western Flyer bicycle down Main Street and had him follow them on his bike the couple blocks to their motel room to question him.

Freddie was confused, scared, and wanted his mother after just a few minutes of questioning. The investigators were in somewhat of a quandary as to whether they should continue their questioning or get his mother. He was after all an adult but mentally a child. It was obvious from the onset that Freddie wasn't bright at all but perhaps they could use his limited capacity to their advantage and get him to confess to killing the child.

After about an hour of questioning, threats, and bullying, Freddie broke down in tears, told the investigators they were mean, and refused to talk to them anymore. Freddie sat in his chair clenching and unclenching his fists and became more and more agitated.

Belweather and Whitfield had a decision to make. Should they restrain him with handcuffs and continue the questioning, contact his mother and allow her to sit in on the interview, or transport him to the county jail for further questioning?

They decided to take him to the county jail. They placed him in their state vehicle and took him to the county jail in Steeleville and left him alone in a cell. As they glared at Freddie through the bars of his cell, they told him they would be back to get the truth out of him. After they left the jailer heard a racket and when he came back to the cell Freddie was beating his head against the bars. The jailer screamed for help and it took three men to restrain Freddie who by that point was bleeding profusely from lacerations to his head.

A local doctor was called to the jail and treated Freddie's injuries and told the jailer to restrain the retarded man and contact the investigators, NOW. When the investigators got back to the jail the doctor told them he had known Freddie for years. He was retarded and any confession they might be able to coerce from him wouldn't stand up in court anyway. He gave them some further advice. If they insisted on terrorizing Freddie, he was going to pick up the phone and call Phil Donnelly, his college fraternity brother who just happened to be the Governor of Missouri. The investigators considered their options and decided it would be a good idea to have the doctor contact Mrs. Hempstein and ask her to come and pick up her son. When Mrs. Hempstein was contacted at work, she told the doctor that she didn't have a car and to have the people who took him to Steeleville bring him back and let him have his bicycle. When the doctor told them, what Mrs. Hempstein had said they were all too happy to oblige.

Belweather and Whitfield were at a standstill. They were sure Freddie didn't have anything to do with the murder but on the other hand they had no other suspects. Since they had been sent to Dogwood to find a killer, they had to come up with someone. So, they decided to watch Freddie's activities and see if there was any compelling reason to bring him in for further questioning.

The next day Freddie went back to his grass cutting job and hoped the bad men wouldn't bother him anymore.

# Chapter 23

Two days after Freddie was released from the county jail, he rode his Western Flyer up to Hiney Swint's pool hall and went inside to get a soda pop. No one would sell alcohol to Freddie, but he would stop in local taverns and pool halls for his Nehi cream soda.

\*\*\*\*\*\*\*\*\*\*\*\*\*\*\*\*\*\*\*\*\*\*\*\*\*\*\*\*\*\*\*\*\*\*\*\*\*\*

In 1924, Chero-Cola added its Nehi line of flavored drinks. The soft drinks became so popular that they outsold all other Chero-Cola beverages. In 1928, Chero-Cola changed its name to the Nehi Corporation. In 1955, Nehi changed its name to Royal Crown Company but continued to bottle its most popular drinks. Whenever Dad would go to Les Collins store to "pump" gasoline, he would take Ken and me along and sometimes buy us a Nehi soda.

\*\*\*\*\*\*\*\*\*\*\*\*\*\*\*\*\*\*\*\*\*\*\*\*\*\*\*\*\*\*\*\*\*\*\*\*\*\*

Pete Stilwell was in the pool hall drinking his and several other people's share of Stag beer when Freddie came into the room. Pete immediately lit into him and called him a child killer and a retard. Freddie got upset and told Pete to leave him alone or he would whup him.

Pete left the pool hall only to return a couple minutes later with his Remington Wingmaster .12-gauge shotgun and pumped two loads of buckshot into Freddie. He watched through bleary eyes as the giant with a child's mind bled out on the floor.

Stilwell was arrested and charged with murder. The charges were pleaded down to manslaughter based on the fact Freddie had threatened Stilwell and another mitigating factor was that Stilwell was drunk. Guess it never occurred to the judge that drunk was Pete Stilwell's normal condition.

Stilwell was taken to the Missouri State Penitentiary in Jefferson City, Missouri, where he was to serve a twenty-year sentence. Stilwell spent most of his time in prison causing arguments and fights. Unfortunately, Stilwell tripped and fell down a flight of steel steps breaking his neck. There was the general opinion someone had helped Stilwell fall or perhaps had broken his neck and then tossed him down the stairs but there wasn't much of an investigation into the incident. Why overwork the staff on an inquiry regarding the alleviation of a problem.

# Chapter 24

Jim Hanes and Bob Graham were squirrel hunting just outside the city limits of Steeleville, Missouri, and hadn't had any luck. Jim was walking ahead of Bob using the theory that a squirrel would circle back around the tree as he passed and allow Bob to get a shot. The problem was there didn't seem to be any squirrels. They were walking in a slow circular motion and after a few minutes Bob and Jim changed positions which would allow Jim to get a shot if they flushed a squirrel.

When Bob entered a slight clearing, he saw George Gable sitting with his back to a tree with a small boy beside him who was crying. Gable was a senior at Steeleville High School and the best basketball player on the team. Being the biggest fish in a small tank wasn't really anything to brag about but Gable was the big guy on campus. Bob asked the little boy what was wrong and got nothing of value in the way of a response, just some whimpering.

Bob asked the boy "Do you want to go home?" And the little boy nodded his head in the affirmative. Bob went forward and took the child by the hand and told Jim to stay with Gable and that as soon as he contacted the sheriff, he would tell him what was going on and try to get the boy to his parents.

Sheriff Dills was in his office when Bob got to town and told the sheriff what they had discovered and asked if he knew the little boy. Dills didn't know him but called Melanie Jackson, the dispatcher, and asked her if she had ever seen the child. Her reply was "Sure, he attends my church with his parents every Sunday morning." Melanie told the sheriff that the little boy was one of the children of the Harris family.

George Harris worked at Earl's Chevrolet as a mechanic. He was contacted and came to the sheriff's office. In the presence of Mr. Harris, Sheriff Dills asked the boy, who was named Tommy, if Gable had hurt him and why he was with him. Tommy responded that Gable had walked by his yard and told him that there was an Indian burial ground in the woods that he wanted to show him. Since he knew Gable went to the high school and he had seen him play basketball he didn't see a problem, so he went with him hoping to find some arrowheads.

After Tommy and Gable walked into the woods a little ways Gable stopped and sat down against a tree, pulled Tommy down beside him, and started hugging him. Tommy was immediately scared and asked Gable to let him go and told him that he wanted to go home. About that time two men with rifles walked up and one took him to the sheriff's office.

Sheriff Dills had dispatched one of the deputies to the wooded area and had taken George Gable into custody for questioning. Gable was placed in an interview room and left there in the presence of a deputy. Gable was a couple months shy of his eighteenth birthday. Dills understood that the law was kind of fuzzy as to whether he needed to notify Gable's parents. Going on the "better safe than sorry" plan, Dills had the dispatcher call Gable's father who worked at the feed mill. Adam Gable showed up and the first words out of his mouth were "What the hell have you gotten yourself into now, George?"

Sheriff Dills explained the situation to Adam Gable and said that he would like his permission to question George but was going to do so with or without permission. Gable's response was, "Why ask my permission if you are going to do what you want to do anyway?"

Dills replied, "Just giving you an opportunity to cooperate." Sheriff Dills then proceeded to question George in the presence of his father and got nothing out of the boy. George Gable just sat and refused to say anything at all. Since Tommy Harris was about the same age as Johnny Blue, he decided to call the state investigators. Sheriff Dills was asked to hold the Gable boy and the investigators would be in Steeleville by the end of the day. Jonas Belweather and Sidney Whitfield loaded into their state vehicle and headed out.

About 4 PM Belweather and Whitfield arrived from the state criminal investigation division at the sheriff's office and got a briefing from Sheriff Dills. Jim Hanes and Bob Graham were contacted, asked to come back to the sheriff's office and were questioned by the state investigators. Bob Graham was asked what he had seen when he encountered Gable and the little boy.

Graham stated, "Nothing other than the boy seemed scared and was crying." They then asked Jim Hanes what Gable had said while they were waiting for the sheriff's deputy to arrive.

Hanes said, "Gable said absolutely nothing to me." After asking Hanes and Graham if they had anything to add and receiving a negative response, the investigators thanked them for coming in and said they were free to leave.

Sheriff Dills had a deputy bring George Gable to the interrogation room where he was confronted by the two state investigators. Adam Gable, the boy's father, declined to sit in on the interrogation and didn't request an attorney be present. They got started with the questioning process about 5 PM and asked questions about Tommy Harris and Johnny Blue Lambert until about 10 PM. They then got Gable a coke and took a break for about thirty minutes. Then they started again. The questions kept going back to what Gable had done with Johnny Blue Lambert. The escapade with the Harris boy seemed of little interest to the investigators.

Around 6 AM the investigators had convinced themselves of two things; Gable was very confused about his sexuality and didn't know beans about the disappearance of Johnny Blue Lambert. The investigators went to the Steeleville Café, ate breakfast, returned to the sheriff's office, and briefed Sheriff Dills. Their conclusion was that George Gable was a pedophile in the making and should be closely monitored to make sure he didn't molest a child. There was little doubt in their mind Gable would have molested the Harris boy had the two hunters not happened on them.

After the debriefing the investigators left, drove to Dogwood, spent the day at the Dogwood Hotel and got some much-needed sleep before driving back to Jefferson City and filing their report. They had nothing to show for their trip to Steeleville but another dead end.

\*\*\*\*\*\*\*\*\*\*\*\*\*\*\*\*\*\*\*\*\*\*\*\*\*\*\*\*\*\*\*\*\*\*\*\*\*\*\*\*\*

Now as Paul Harvey would say, "For the rest of the story." After graduation from high school, George Gable attended Holy Cross College in Notre Dame, Indiana. After graduating from Holy Cross, Gable went into the priesthood and in due time was promoted to Bishop. When a parent caught Father Gable in the act of molesting her son at Saint Andrew the Apostle Catholic Church near Chicago, Illinois, all hell broke loose in the diocese. The leader of the archdiocese punted the problem upstairs to the Cardinal who resided in Chicago, Illinois. After sending a bishop to investigate the allegations, the cardinal worked out a deal with the archdiocese of Denver, Colorado. Bishop Gable was demoted and transferred to Colorado Springs, Colorado, so that he could molest children on a high elevation. Perhaps if Father Gable was a mile closer to God, he would tone down his despicable acts.

# Chapter 25

Bradford Johnstone came home from the Korean War without a scratch and decided to stay in the army. When he came back to the states, he was assigned to Fort Benning, Georgia, to the Airborne Department, in The Infantry School. After he completed his training, he was assigned to the 6th Armored Division, Fort Leonard Wood, Saint Robert, Missouri, as a technical instructor. In 1956 the facility was renamed as the U.S. Army Training Center Engineer.

Fort Leonard Wood is about fifty miles south of Dogwood on Highway 66 (Interstate 44). Sergeant Johnstone would drive to Dogwood and stay with his parents on most of those weekends when he didn't have assigned duty. On one of those trips, he was at Hoyt McCann's pool hall, shooting pool, and drinking more Stag beer than he should have, and started bragging about his service in Korea.

According to Johnstone's intoxicated story, he was on a patrol with five other soldiers, came to a small village, and found a North Korean flag in one of the huts. Bradford claimed that he and the patrol killed all the gooks in the village, including women and children, and never reported the incident to the Army. One of the older men in the tavern and pool room overheard Bradford and found the act of killing civilians reprehensible. He had been in Italy during World War II and believed in adherence to the rules of war.

The veteran, Homer Swindell, called the Fort Leonard Wood fort commander to report what he had overheard. The general wasn't in but Colonel Jackson, his Executive Officer, took notes and thanked Mr. Swindell for his call. Colonel Jackson contacted Colonel Smith, the Provost Marshall, who in turn contacted the Army Criminal Investigation Division (CID). A criminal investigator from Fort Benning, Columbus, Georgia, was assigned the case. He took a train to Saint Louis, Missouri, rented an automobile, drove to Lebanon, Missouri, turned in the rental car, and was picked up by a lieutenant from the provost marshal office.

After calling the Fort Leonard Wood commander, Swindell had called Sheriff Dills and told him about what he had heard. Dills thanked Swindell and contemplated what implication if any a killing in Korea might have with the murder of a child in Dogwood. Sheriff Dills asked Swindell if he could remember the date he had overheard the conversation. Swindell was certain of the date, and if he was correct, it was after Johnny Blue's body had been found.

Jeremy Smithers was the name of the CID investigator and he was assigned a billet at Fort Leonard Wood and unpacked his suitcase. The lieutenant left the government vehicle with Mr. Smithers and got an enlisted man to come pick him up.

The following morning Smithers went to the officer's club, ate breakfast and then went to the provost marshal office to be briefed. After the briefing, Smithers requested that Sergeant Johnstone be brought to the provost marshal office to be questioned. Smithers questioned Johnstone all day and then allowed him to go to the chow hall under Military Police escort and then he was returned to the provost marshal office.

Smithers took a break and went back to the officer's club for dinner. About 6 PM Smithers renewed the questioning and around 10 PM Sergeant Johnstone broke down and confessed and implicated the other soldiers who were on the patrol with him.

At the request of Sheriff Dills, Smithers had questioned Johnstone extensively after his confession to the murders in Korea concerning the death of the child in Dogwood. Anyone who would kill defenseless women and children was certainly capable of killing a little boy. The investigator's opinion was that Johnstone had no knowledge of the murder and felt, given the man's traumatic state, he would have confessed if he was involved with the crime.

Nothing of consequence was uncovered concerning the murder of Johnny Blue but the Army did have a mess to deal with. And to their credit, they court martialed Johnstone and the others responsible for the massacre.

\*\*\*\*\*\*\*\*\*\*\*\*\*\*\*\*\*\*\*\*\*\*\*\*\*\*\*\*\*\*\*\*\*\*\*\*\*\*\*

History tends to repeat itself and basically the same type of massacre occurred at a village named My Lai in South Vietnam during the Vietnamese War.

A company of American soldiers killed most of the villagers; women, children, and old men. All in all, more than 500 people were slaughtered in the My Lai massacre on March 16, 1968. Many of the women and girls were raped and mutilated before being killed. U.S. Army officers covered up the carnage for more than a year before someone leaked the story to the press. The brutality of the My Lai killings and the official cover-up added fuel to the anti-war movement and further divided Americans over the war in Vietnam.

Based on the incident at My Lai, former Navy Lieutenant John Forbes Kerry testified before a senate committee and likened American soldiers to Genghis Khan's bloodthirsty exploits. Kerry later parlayed his betrayal of his military comrades into a successful run for the senate seat in Massachusetts and a failed attempt to become President of the United States.

Kerry confirmed that, when taking out the trash, rich Ne'er-do-wells with political ambitions shouldn't be excluded!

# Chapter 26

The man who killed Johnny Blue put on rubber gloves and wrapped the boy's body in a packing blanket and put him inside the door of the house. The two men then wiped down everything solid or metal within the rental house with Clorox soaked rags trying to make sure they left no fingerprints or other evidence which might tie them to the abduction of the little girl. They then went into the basement and used a garbage bag to suffocate the girl and wrapped her in another of the cheap blankets.

Just before 2 AM they loaded the two dead children in the Chevrolet panel truck and one man went to Main Street and disposed of the boy. The other man, who drove a dark green 1954 Studebaker spread gas around the living and dining rooms of the house, backed to the front door, and flipped a match into the room. The ground floor was an inferno within just a couple minutes.

The man put the small gasoline can on the floorboard of the Studebaker, drove off to get on Route 66 East, and then crossed over to I-44 towards St. Louis at the first interchange.

After the man driving the panel truck placed Johnny Blue's body in the storm drain, he went out Highway 19 to Interstate 44 and headed east towards St. Louis. The two men met for coffee at the Diamonds Restaurant in Villa Ridge, Missouri, and discussed what if anything might incriminate them concerning the killing of the boy, the little girl, or the torching of the rental house. This wasn't their first rodeo regarding abducting a little girl and having a few days of fun before making her go away. But it was the first time they had killed anyone without a plan and disposal scheduled. The deed was much more unemotional if it was well planned. Doing things in a responsive manner was upsetting.

The man who had rented the house in Dogwood had used a driver's license of a dead man and he couldn't be traced. He had met the owner of the house only one time and in disguise with a mustache and goatee, and wore a blond wig, so no accurate description of him would be forthcoming. They had left no trail of any kind because they had brought food with them and never went out of the house once they arrived with the little girl. They had backed the automobiles into the driveway so the license plates would be hidden from the street. They had selected the house on Sycamore Street because, after they moved in, it was the only occupied dwelling on the street. All in all, it had been a fun few days and would have lasted longer had it not been for the nosy little boy.

The men ate a leisurely breakfast, shook hands, and went their separate ways. The green Studebaker driver back on I-44 to go to his home in St. Louis and the black Chevrolet panel truck driver left to take care of one more piece of business before returning to Illinois.

# Chapter 27

Shortly after 2 AM the same morning Johnny Blue's body was dumped in the storm drain inlet; the Dogwood volunteer fire department received a call of a house fire on Sycamore Street. The house was fully ablaze when the first fire truck arrived. Despite the best efforts of the firemen, nothing of the house could be saved. Dogwood didn't have a standing fire department and volunteer firefighters had to be called. Then a chain calling procedure was initiated. By the time all that was accomplished, the fire was out of control. The fire truck did arrive in time to see a mighty big fire though.

Try as they might the fire department could never get the fire under control and the house burned to the ground and fell into the basement where it continued to blaze until it burned all its fuel. Since it was the only house on the street at the time, the fire department only used just enough water to make sure the fire didn't spread to other houses on the next streets.

When state fire investigators were notified a house had burned down and the renter couldn't be located, they became interested and sent a state arson team to Dogwood. The arson investigators, John

Smith and Frederick Johnson, discovered gasoline had been used as an accelerant to make sure the fire spread quickly. The arson investigators sifted through the remains of the house and found nothing of interest. The fire had obviously been started on purpose but by whom and for what purpose could not be determined.

The thing the investigators found very interesting was even though some metal objects were still intact, like the refrigerator and stove and water faucets on the kitchen and bathroom sinks, not even a partial fingerprint was recovered from them. It was as if someone had wiped everything clean. Laboratory analysis of the smaller metal objects would reveal a residue of Clorox.

When the arson investigators checked out John Merkel, the owner of the house, they discovered he had worked the night shift at the foundry in West Plains and had gotten off work at midnight. West Plains was 120 miles from Dogwood but the roads to Dogwood weren't exactly interstate quality. When they brought Merkel in for questioning, they hit a brick wall. They were told that after he got off work, he stayed in the parking lot with two co-workers and drank a Falstaff beer before going to his house in West Plains. Merkel gave the investigators the co-workers names and was released to file his insurance claim on the house on Sycamore Street. When the investigators went to West Plains, they confirmed Merkel's story of drinking the beer and shooting the bull with the two co-workers. They also went by his small house in West Plains and met a neighbor who had seen Merkel going out to get the morning paper about 6 AM. He knew it was about 6 AM on the morning in question because he saw John go out every morning about 6 AM and get his newspaper off the lawn to read as he was having his morning coffee.

Obviously, the homeowner hadn't started the fire that destroyed the house. He might have had motive because of living in another town and only renting the house in Dogwood sporadically but finding some local person who might have started the fire on Merkel's behalf would be impossible. The investigators had questioned several people who had started house fires or hired someone to do it for them and if Merkel was guilty of destroying the house, he was the best liar they had ever met.

When they tried to follow up on the man who had rented the house, they ran into another brick wall. Everything about the man was a ruse. The driver's license was fraudulent and the address the man used was a vacant lot.

The investigators closed the file with the fire being started by person or persons unknown, but they wondered if something much more sinister than a common house fire had occurred on Sycamore Street in Dogwood. There was just too much about the entire scenario which didn't make sense on any level. There was more to this than met the eye. They just didn't know what it was.

# Chapter 28

The black panel truck pulled off old Route 66 just before getting to Marlborough, Missouri, and entered a county blacktop road. Then after driving about five miles the driver turned onto a gravel farm lane and began to relax. He was just never sure they were going to be able to get away with the abduction of a young girl and a wonderful sexual experience until everything was completely tidied up. The possibility of something unplanned happening was always a possibility. A flat tire, being stopped by a cop for any reason, or an accident was always possible even though extremely improbable. The driver could never relax until he had completely sanitized the black panel truck and returned to his home.

When he pulled up to the clapboard farmhouse, he could see the old 1949 Wain-Roy backhoe sitting in the middle of the field. As he pulled up, the hole was ready. The man had dug it about six feet deep, three feet wide and about five feet long. The driver took the blanket with its cargo and dumped it into the waiting hole. While the farmer was sitting on the backhoe smoking a cigarette, the truck driver took the Kansas license plate off the panel truck and threw it into the hole.

The panel truck driver handed the Wain-Roy driver a cigar box containing $250.00 in ten and twenty dollar bills and waved goodbye. As he drove off the farmer cranked up the Wain-Roy and began backfilling the hole.

The driver of the panel truck waited until he was out of sight of the backhoe driver and stopped and put his Illinois license plate on the truck. He then wiped down every area of the truck he could reach with a Clorox soaked rag. There was no blood and the girl's clothes were in the blanket with the body. He had no idea what forensic experts could find but he was taking no chances.

This was the farmer's fourth hole in three years. He never asked any questions and didn't want to know what the man wanted buried. He had been told they were financial records which could be incriminating if discovered by the Internal Revenue Service. The $250.00 certainly augmented his small income from farming and there was no other way he could make $250.00 for a few hours' work. He just dug the holes when told to do so, backfilled them with dirt, and harrowed over them to obscure the fact there had been anything done to the soil of the field. He didn't like the federal government much anyway, so burying records which could get the man in trouble seemed like a patriotic act of defiance.

\*\*\*\*\*\*\*\*\*\*\*\*\*\*\*\*\*\*\*\*\*\*\*\*\*\*\*\*\*\*\*\*\*\*\*\*\*\*\*\*\*\*

The green Studebaker pulled into the driveway of a house in O'Fallon, Missouri, pulled into the garage, took the Kansas plates off the car and replaced them with his Missouri license plates. He then took a box of assorted junk off a shelf, folded the license plate, placed it in the box and took it to the trash can on the curb. Ellen would be home from work in a few hours and the girls would be home from school about 3 PM. So, he took a shower, read the morning paper and waited to tell them of his success on his business meeting in Topeka, Kansas.

\*\*\*\*\*\*\*\*\*\*\*\*\*\*\*\*\*\*\*\*\*\*\*\*\*\*\*\*\*\*\*\*\*\*\*\*\*\*\*\*\*\*

The black Chevrolet panel truck pulled into the apartment complex in Washington Park, Illinois, and parked in its assigned spot. The man went into the apartment he shared with his elderly mother, kissed her on the cheek, and told her he had enjoyed a wonderful short vacation. He took his garment bag to the laundry room and put his clothes into the washing machine. Then he put on his robe and slippers and asked his mom if she would like to go out for dinner or did she want him to make something special?

\*\*\*\*\*\*\*\*\*\*\*\*\*\*\*\*\*\*\*\*\*\*\*\*\*\*\*\*\*\*\*\*\*\*\*\*\*\*

They had been lucky but preparation and intricate planning always had produced luck. The little boy was an unexpected problem, but they had worked through it. They would wait a few months and find another suitable house, a pretty little girl and play their game again. There were lots of little girls……

# Chapter 29

At 9 PM on December 22, 1963, I walked out of my part-time job with Hecht Department Store in Suitland, Maryland, got in my 1962 Plymouth convertible, and headed for Missouri. The Hecht stores were later bought out by the Macy's chain. I drove all night and arrived in Dogwood, Missouri, around noon on the 23rd to spend Christmas with my parents and brother Ken.

On the afternoon of the 26th I left for Bolling AFB, Washington, D.C. where my bachelor quarters were located. Shortly before midnight on the 26th, I fell asleep while driving and turned my car over several times. Fortunately, I was wearing the seat belt in the car; something I had never done before. I woke up as the car left the road and everything from that point on was a complete blur.

When I awoke, I found myself in a hospital bed with my mother sitting in a chair by my bedside. It seems that I had suffered a brain concussion and had been in a coma for two days. Once I gained my senses, I looked at mom and asked; "Did they ever catch whoever killed Johnny Blue Lambert?"

Mom looked at me like I was from another planet and replied, "Honey, the

Lambert boy is the star athlete for the Dogwood High School basketball team. I was just reading about him a few days ago in the Dogwood Times. He isn't dead."

The neurologist came into my room during mid-morning. When Mom told him about my strange questions, the doctor said, "Sergeant, you suffered a condition called "reality disorientation" while in the coma. That is a condition were real things, people, and events are combined with events your mind contrives. Over time, you will be able to sort out what was real and what your mind invented while you were in the coma."

I retired from the Air Force in April 1981 and went to work in the construction industry with Daniel/Fluor Corporation.

I later resigned and built cabinets and custom furniture in North Florida, did accounting work, and was involved with the tomato business. I now devote my time to writing books, traveling around the country, and fly fishing when I have the opportunity.

The constant is that I still have trouble at times with the dream I had while in the coma. How much of the dream was true and how much was concocted by my mind? The strange thing is that a house on Sycamore Street did burn down in 1956! The ambiguity between truth and fiction is what makes an interesting story.

# Chapter 30

On April 17, 1957 Melba Johnson called the Peoria, Illinois, Police Department and reported that a dark panel truck had driven through her neighborhood at least a half dozen times in the past two days. The desk sergeant figured that it was just a nervous old lady with nothing to occupy her mind but sent a patrol cruiser to investigate.

While driving to the neighborhood, the deputy saw a dark gray Chevrolet panel truck sitting at a railroad crossing. He decided he would check the vehicle driver's operator's license. When the deputy neared the panel truck, he put on his warning lights and siren. The panel truck accelerated through the flashing warning lights and got broadsided by an oncoming passenger train. The panel truck exploded into a ball of fire.

The coroner did dental impressions to identify the two bodies. Within a couple weeks both bodies had been identified. One was Samuel Riveria of Washington Park, Illinois, and the passenger was Jefferson Jackson of O'Fallon, Missouri. There were no wants or warrants for either man. However, the panel truck had a stolen Illinois license plate. On the 18th, the owner of the Sleep Well Inn called the Peoria Police

Department to report an abandoned 1954 green Studebaker.

"… **Vengeance** is **mine**; I will repay, saith **the LORD**." Romans 12:19

# Epilogue

According to the National Center for Missing and Exploited Children which cites Department of Justice reports, nearly 800,000 children are reported missing each year. This is more than 2,000 per day.

There are three distinct types of kidnapping: kidnapping by a relative of the victim or "family kidnapping" (49 percent), kidnapping by an acquaintance of the victim or "acquaintance kidnapping" (27 percent), and kidnapping by a stranger to the victim or "stranger kidnapping" (24 percent).

Stranger kidnapping victimizes more females than males, occurs primarily at outdoor locations, victimizes both teenagers and school-age children, is associated with sexual assaults in the case of girl victims and robberies in the case of boy victims (although not exclusively so), and is the type of kidnapping most likely to involve the use of a firearm.

About twenty percent of the children reported to the National Center for Missing and Exploited Children in nonfamily abductions are not found alive.

One child who is robbed of his or her life is one too many!!

**Bill Shuey** is the author of several books and the weekly ObverseView column. He travels extensively in his recreational vehicle with his wife, Gloria, and his fly rods.

He can be contacted at:
billshueybooks@gmail.com
www.billshueybooks.com

Made in the USA
Columbia, SC
07 January 2020